PISCES

ZODIAC KILLERS #4

WL KNIGHTLY

BRIXBAXTER PUBISHING

Pisces

Copyright © 2018 by W.L. Knightly

First Edition.

Editor: Eric Martinez
Cover Art: Kellie Dennis at Book Cover by Design

1

FINN

Finn had thought that coming to New York was going to be the trip that made all of his dreams come true, in more ways than one. But so far, it had been an emotional shitstorm, and he was ready to cut anchor and head back home. As he sat on the end of his hotel bed, pulling on his shoes and listening to Edie on the other end of the phone in LA talk about her latest purchase for her boutique, he looked up to the statue of the steampunk heart and thought of Logan sitting alone somewhere in a jail cell.

"Are you even listening to me?" Edie's tone sharpened, bringing his full attention back to her ramblings.

"Yes, of course, I am. I'm trying to get my shoes on so I can get down to Bay's office. There's a lot going on here."

"Like what? You never tell me what's going on, and you know I'm dying to know if I'm going to be your fashion coordinator for the movie."

"Yes, trust me, you're a shoe-in, but if I don't get time to work these investors, which you know I hate, there won't be any fucking movie."

"You're such a grumpy puppy," she said in her sweetest voice, which he also hated. It always reminded Finn of the way people talked to small children and babies, and he was neither. "I talked to Mother, and she said that if you still want to use the garden for a few scenes, you can, but she is going to have you pay the gardening fees for the month, plus a bonus so that Pedro isn't upset."

"Of course, she wants me to pay. The point is, I need someone to trust that I won't destroy their fucking garden and let me do it for free, but that's fine. I'll think about it. I might just change the scene to a fucking park."

"Don't stress over it, sweetie. I'll talk to Mother, and I'm sure she'll waive the fee."

"Trust me, that's the least of my worries." He had bigger shit to stress over in life, like making it through the fucking week. There was someone out there targeting Zodiacs, and since he was next in line after Logan Miller, who had already lost two of his girlfriends, both of which he was being accused of killing, things were starting to make him nervous. There was only one person in the world who could give him reassurance, and that was who he was about to go meet up with. "Look, I've got to go, baby. I'm in a bad mood, and I'm afraid I'm not good company."

"It's not a problem, you're a hardworking, creative genius, and I'm really proud of you for finally chasing your dream." He knew what she meant to say was that she was proud of him for finally getting out of his fucking apartment and living life.

Before he'd decided to devote his full attention to making this dream movie a reality, he'd spent the past year of his life holed up in their beach house, growing his hair out and writing the perfect screenplay. His blood, sweat, and tears had gone into it. Edie had been great to encourage him, and while he always wanted his life to be normal for the most part, he couldn't get over feeling like their life together was a lie.

Still, she stood through it all with him, even the long hours of him retreating to hotel rooms where he was "writing" and all the late nights in the sex clubs where he was getting the kind of encouragement that *really* kept him going.

He often felt like he should cut her loose, but she was like his curtain, his façade, and he was afraid if he lost her, then everyone would see him for what he really was: bisexual.

He pushed the thoughts from his mind. Nope, not him. Just because he was attracted to one man, in *love* with one man, even, did not a bisexual make. He'd reminded himself of that logic many times, and a few times, it had even convinced him. He tried not to beat himself up about it. He still enjoyed the company of women and lived his life as a heterosexual man. Most of his trysts never even included men, and when they did, he had never really done more than touch. So, what if he was saving himself for someone in particular? It didn't mean that he was going to get him.

After Finn ended the call, he went down to find his red muscle car had made it through another night in the parking garage, and as he walked around it to make sure it was still pristine, footsteps across the lot brought his head up. He hurried and got into his car, and once he had it started, he saw a woman in his rearview fishing out her keys.

He headed across town, and when he got to Bay's office, he walked in and found a smiling receptionist. Bay never had anyone ugly working for him, and as Finn looked at the woman's perfect mouth, he couldn't help but wonder if it had ever been wrapped around Bay's huge cock.

"I'm here to see Bay Collins," he said.

"He's not in yet, but he's on his way. You can head up to his office if you like. There's a small bench outside his door. He'll be right up."

Bay's office was designed for privacy, and he wondered if there would be anyone else waiting on the bench for him this morning. "Thank you."

He went into the elevator and heard Bay's voice behind him. "Hold that, please."

Finn turned around in the elevator to see Bay's receptionist get up and rush to the elevator doors. Finn held it open, but she clamped her hand over the door, too.

Bay strode over and smiled at the woman. "Thank you, sweetheart." His words were like praise to the woman, and she blushed as she turned and walked away. Bay climbed in the elevator beside Finn, and the doors shut.

"Sweetheart?" Finn asked. "Let me guess. You're fucking her, too?" Finn tried not to sound so jaded, but it didn't work. He leaned against the wall as the elevator moved.

"Careful, Finn. Someone might think you're jealous." Bay turned his head and gave him a devilish grin. Of every man in the world, why did Finn have to want *him*? Someone who was completely and utterly unattainable.

Finn couldn't even dignify him with a response. "Is it true that you're defending Logan?"

Bay nodded. "Yes, it is. Along with Katherine Fallwell. She's going to be on his defense team in the trial. I just came from seeing him, actually."

"How's he doing?"

The elevator stopped, and when the door opened, he allowed Bay to go first, not only so he could stare at his perfect ass and the confident way he moved, but because the man needed to unlock the office door.

Bay took out his key and worked the lock, and this time, when the door opened, he stepped aside and held the door for Finn. "He's doing well. Already institutionalized."

Bay walked around and offered Finn a seat. Then he went to the other side of his desk and sat in his big, black leather chair that was more like a throne. Finn knew the man was in control of his world and ruled it like no one else he knew.

"I hope he's okay," Finn said. "Do you think he'll make it?"

"I'm sure he'll manage, but probably not as good as you would since he's not used to being on his knees like you are."

Finn assumed it was a joke, but he just shifted in his seat, uncomfortable. "I guess you'd know?"

"Stop being so transparent. I'm sure you didn't come down here to talk about Logan's well-being."

"I did, actually. But I also wanted to know if I'm safe."

"I don't know, are you?" Bay asked.

"Stop it. You know what I fucking mean." He pulled down his V-neck to show the brand on his shoulder which looked like a strange H. "Do I have to fucking worry now that someone is coming after me? I'm next, right?"

"Relax, if they're coming after anyone, it's still Logan. He thinks he's safe, but there are ways to get to people in the pen. Once he's transferred down to County, he'll see just how tough it really is. Then he'll wish he was down here on his fucking knees for me." He tapped his desk.

Finn crossed his arms and turned his head to look out the window. "Funny, but it doesn't do a damned thing to comfort me. This entire trip has been a nightmare, and I'm still one investor short. I had hoped to secure enough to give me the green light on this new movie."

"Ah, yes, that reminds me," Bay said. "In light of Logan not being involved anymore, I am rethinking my offer."

Finn's heart sank. "Please, Bay. Don't do this to me. You're all I have. You know I need you."

"Yeah, so much you spent six grand on a fucking heart statue." Bay's expression dared him to deny it.

"How do you even know about that?" He didn't think Logan had told anyone about that.

"Eyes and ears everywhere." Bay took out his phone and showed Finn surveillance from the inside of Logan's studio.

"Do you have my hotel room bugged, too?" He knew Bay was crazy, but he had no idea the lengths he had gone to.

Bay grinned. "Yeah, I do, and if you could stop screaming my name when you masturbate, I'd really appreciate it." There was a moment of awkward pause as Finn tried to remember what the fuck he was talking about, but Bay laughed. "I'm only kidding, but thanks for that. The look on your face told me all I needed to know." He shook his head and put his phone back in his pocket.

"You're really upset about me spending my own money? I didn't cash your check for Logan. I sent it back. That was out of my personal account, not the movie account."

"That's just it. How much of your own money are you investing in this mockumentary you're making?"

"It's not a mockumentary. It's a fantasy piece set up to be like a real documentary, but there's nothing mocking about it. I've explained it to you, and believe it or not, I'm using a lot of my own money, and Edie's, but I have bills to pay until this thing pays off. Look, are you on board or not?" He needed to know if he was wasting his time.

"I'll think about it." Bay's nonchalant attitude was driving him crazy. "But I wouldn't stop looking for investors."

"Look, don't leave me hanging, man. I have to get my shit together, and if I can't, then I want to get the fuck out of here." He wasn't going to waste another minute of his time if Bay wasn't on board.

"What's wrong with New York?" Bay swiveled in his chair back and forth, like a cat twitching its tail.

"There's a fucking killer out there." Finn waved his hand to the window.

"And your point is?" Bay laughed. "Lighten up. And don't worry. I'll let you know."

"I'm meeting Raven tonight, and we're going down to Taunt. I was hoping you and your lady would come and join us."

Bay kept up the swiveling, his eyes narrowing in a seductive way as he eyed Finn. "I don't know. I'd like to, but I'm punishing Lila."

"There's no better punishment than to make her watch someone else serve you." Finn licked his lips, but Bay laughed.

"I suppose you want that honor?" Bay could be a real bitch when he wanted to be.

Finn pegged him with a hard stare. "No, I didn't say that. I'm bringing Raven."

"Does Edie care if you're hooking up in sex clubs while she's back home being the princess to her mommy and daddy's kingdom?"

"What she doesn't know won't hurt her. Besides, she's so missionary it's boring, and I get tired of tasting vanilla if you know what I mean."

Bay gave him a smug grin. "I know better than anyone. I guess what I'm asking you is, does she know about your dark desires?"

"No. Hell no. She's never understood that. Besides, I'm over it." It had been years before, and even though he'd wanted it every day since, Bay didn't need to know that.

Bay laughed. "Yeah, we'll see."

"So, do you want to go or not?" He knew that he and Bay would have a lot of fun with Raven.

"I don't know. I guess you'll find out if I show up."

Finn could have kicked himself for even asking. He didn't know why he continued to torture himself for Bay Collins. The guy had always had too much power over him from the very first day they met, and even though Finn knew that they were probably never going to have another special time together like they did when they were younger, he couldn't help but want it to happen again.

"Fine, I'll let you know what I find out about the other investor, and hopefully I'll see you tonight. Either way, me and Raven will be there." He got up and showed himself out. Then, as he entered the elevator, he called Raven.

"Hey, lover." Her voice was thick and sexy, and Finn's cock stiffened at the thought of the last time he'd had her.

"I just wanted to make sure you're still on for tonight at Taunt." He didn't want to have to find another woman to go, but he would if need be. He was still holding out hope that Bay and his wife would show up.

"You know it. I'm counting the minutes. I even shined up my favorite pair of boots. You came all over them that one night."

"I was giving them a high-shine waxing. I bet they sparkle." He remembered how hot that night had been, and he'd wondered whatever happened to those boots.

She giggled and then gave a little moan. "I hope I make you do that again."

"I'm sure you will. I'll see you tonight, babe." He ended the call and then took a deep breath as he headed out of the elevator and said a prayer. With any luck, the rest of his day would go smoothly.

2

DAREK

Darek's back was screaming as he sat behind the wheel of his partner Lizzy's Land Rover. The usually comfortable seats weren't doing him any favors, and now he was regretting that they hadn't stopped off in Maryland on the way to Virginia. Instead, Lizzy wanted to drive on through and check into a hotel.

They were on the road and getting close to the old diner. Darek wondered if it had changed much.

Lizzy was staring down at her phone. "There should be a diner up here according to my GPS, and when we get there, let's go ahead and check it out. I'm hungry, and I need to stretch my legs."

They rounded a bend in the road, and the diner came into view. It had indeed changed a lot. The name of it was Gas and Guzzle now. The two gas pumps it used to have out front had been replaced with a huge twenty-pump station, and the diner looked more like a convenience store.

Darek knew he had to act like he'd never been there. "Is this it?"

"Yeah, it's not quite what I was expecting either." Lizzy unbuckled her seatbelt and then gave him an apologetic look. "I'm hitting the little girls' room before we go out back."

"Are you sure this is the place? There's a barbecue restaurant inside."

Lizzy nodded. "This is the address. I guess a lot has changed. If we're lucky, we'll find some of the same old staff."

She hurried in, and Darek took a minute to check his phone, which had made a few sounds while he was driving. He also checked the burner phone, which was the only direct line of communication he had with the killer. While the last message was still there to haunt him, there was nothing new.

The words from the last message still surprised him. Whoever the killer was, they'd had a hard time ripping poor Lidia Hobbs to shreds, and he figured that was why the killing had been so brutal. It was more deliberate and forced. The person had to muster up everything in them, and they probably weren't even watching what they were doing. They'd hacked into her until she was nearly bisected.

The phone vibrated in his hand, causing him to jump. When he looked down at the message, it was from the killer. "*Have a nice trip,*" he read aloud. "Really? So now the killer is a fucking smart ass to boot? Just wonderful."

He glanced around and wondered if they could have been followed, but it was ridiculous to think that way. Someone in the department might have run their mouth, or the killer had seen them leaving with their bags.

Darek stowed the phone away and returned his focus to the task at hand. He couldn't believe that the diner was no more. He wondered if the same family owned and operated the place. Maybe they had expanded their business from the mom and pop type location to a national franchise.

He walked in, and the bell on the door still sounded the same, but the place didn't bring back any memories. That was a good thing, but he wasn't sure it was going to do him any favors. He might not have any horrible flashbacks here, but he still hadn't made it to Camp Victory. That little walk down memory lane still kept him awake at night.

Lizzy walked out of the bathroom and joined him near the fountain drinks dispensers. "Do you want to sit down and have something to eat?"

"Let's grab a sandwich and get back on the road. The day isn't getting any younger and we're burning daylight." Darek didn't want to sit around in case he saw anyone that remembered him when he was just a kid. It was unlikely but possible, so better safe than sorry.

"Then let's go ahead and order," she said. "We can look around outside while we wait."

"Sure." He kept his head down as he ordered, even though the girl taking his order wasn't anyone he'd know. He glanced at some of the other employees and didn't see a single person he remembered from the old days.

Once they ordered and Lizzy explained who they were and what they were doing, the manager wanted to walk out with them and insisted on giving them a law enforcement discount, which he ended up making free.

"You're looking into that case where they found that girl?" The man walked them out to the back. "I heard she was found out here. That old boy they convicted, he died. I've had a few people tell me this place is haunted by her."

"Haunted?" Lizzy's back stiffened. "Do you know any real facts or is it just urban legend?"

"Well, some people think it's true." He shrugged. "I heard that old boy said he was innocent, but I think he should have fried. Dying in prison was too good for him for what he did."

"Does *he* haunt your business, too?" Darek asked. He could tell that Lizzy wasn't too impressed with the man's contributions, and she gave him a sour look for encouraging the manager.

She took off to the edge of the woods, following the information she'd gotten from the report. "The body was found more in this area, at least according to the file. It almost seems like whoever put her here probably hadn't realized there was a diner there at all."

Darek caught up, with the manager on his heels. The man was anxious, as if he might miss something. "That's why they think

Gough put her here," he said. "He found her; he had to have known she was back here. If you ask me, he did it."

Lizzy gave him a sour look and read through part of the police report. Then she pointed out into the woods. "There's a fence here. It's not in the report."

Darek hadn't encountered a fence all those years ago. He was trying to keep himself distracted from the image of Emily burning in his brain. In his mind, he was still running through those woods, his feet sloshing through the muck of recent rains as the mist of summer showers fell from the sky.

"We put that up a few months back," the manager said. "Ever since that boys' camp reopened about a mile up the road. I know they were some of the ones up to no good around here. We put up with it for a long time, but after the fire, we just couldn't see letting that happen to this place."

"Fire?" Lizzy and Darek spoke at the same time.

"Yeah." The man acted as though he couldn't believe they didn't know about it. "There was a fire at the main office of the camp."

"What happened?" Darek asked.

"Well, some say it was the boys being rebellious, but I asked my daughter, and she said the kids were talking about tax fraud."

Darek didn't think that sounded like the owners of Camp V, but then, things had changed. Lizzy was visibly shaken by the news, and Darek knew that it was because her hopes for finding more clues were vanishing. He hoped that was the case, but he offered a comforting hand to her back.

"Could you give us a minute?" Darek asked the manager.

"Yeah, sure. I'll just go in and check on those burgers. You two take all the time you need and let me know if you need any more help."

"Thanks," Darek said.

"The name's Albert." He walked away, and Darek turned back to Lizzy.

She smiled. "Thanks for that. He was driving me up the fucking wall. Haunted? Really? How fucking disrespectful."

Darek shrugged. "Yeah, some people are assholes. So, what's next?"

Lizzy looked defeated. "Well, I say we take our dinner and go find a place to stay the night. We'll regroup and try to hit the place first thing tomorrow."

Darek feigned disappointment. "You were looking forward to getting over there."

"Yeah, until numbnuts said the place burned down. What kind of evidence am I going to be able to find if it's burned up?"

Darek was banking on it but decided to offer more comfort. "Maybe it wasn't the main building? Maybe it wasn't that bad." Darek hoped that the entire place had been burned down to ashes so he could put this part of his life behind him and focus on anything else that might help them find the new killer. The old evidence wasn't going to do anything but expose him and the other Zodiacs.

"I don't want to know tonight," she said. "I know it sounds bad, but I'm so fucking upset that I don't want to even go there until I have time to process this. Not only that, but no one said a word about there being a fire when I called. I should make them pay the state for this trip." She rolled her eyes and crossed her arms.

Darek tried not to smile as he pulled her into his arms. "Let's get those burgers. We'll come back here later, and maybe we can figure something out."

"I wanted to see if I could walk from here to the camp." She turned and looked at the damned fence and her brows furrowed. "Stupid fence."

"At least you know it wasn't there back then." He tried to offer what he could without incriminating himself and knew she deserved a better partner.

"Right. Come on." She waved her hand at Darek and then walked back to the building. They were greeted by Albert who had a greasy paper bag with their names on it.

"Thank you for your help, and we appreciate the burgers." Lizzy snatched up the sack, and Darek gave the man an apologetic look.

"Here." The man reached over the counter for two large plastic cups. "Get yourself a drink on the way out."

"Will do." Darek gave him a toothy grin and thanked him as he took the cups. He paused to fill them up as Lizzy went back out to her Rover.

"You could have been a tad more pleasant," he said as he caught up to her. "He gave us our food."

"I know, I'm sorry. I'm just frustrated. What if we've come all this way for nothing?"

"I don't think we did. Let's get on the road, find our hotel, and regroup." The longer he put off going to the camp, the better. Even if it had changed and was nothing more than a dead end, that was okay by him.

"Okay, but I'm eating in the car, so you're still driving." She walked around and climbed into the passenger seat.

Darek opened the door and climbed into the driver's seat. She was already munching on a French fry and unwrapping her burger. "Fine, but I'm eating, too, so I don't want one word about my shitty driving."

"Deal." She put the bag on the center console and then took a bite of the burger.

"How is it?"

Her eyes rolled back in her head, and he wished he could make her react that way as she moaned. "Worth the trip."

He hoped that wasn't the only pleasure they got out of it.

3

FINN

Taunt had a good crowd for once, not the busy, overcrowded scene it usually was. Raven looked amazing as usual. He didn't know how he'd gotten lucky enough to hook up with such a perfect companion. She was everything he wanted and needed in a partner for this kind of place, and her confidence made her even hotter.

They were there not ten minutes when a familiar man caught his attention in the distance. Seth Stone was still as hot as he'd been when they were younger, but Finn wasn't sure his tastes were. He took Raven's hand and led her across the room to where Seth and a woman who might have been all of nineteen were ordering drinks.

Like all the Zodiacs, Seth had a special wristband. "Seth?"

"Finn? Hey, man. It's good to see you." He turned his eyes to Raven and gave her the once-over. "This is my wife, Kari. Darling, this is Finn. He's an old friend."

"Nice to meet you." Kari looked him up and down as she licked her lips.

"It's nice to meet you. This is Raven. She's my guest for the evening. We're looking for some fun."

Seth smiled, and Finn's cock hardened. He remembered a particular afternoon from when they were younger. They'd once shared a shower stall at Camp V, which wasn't anything out of the ordinary because they had too many boys and not enough stalls, and no one wanted to take all day and be last in the chow line. Seth had hidden a picture of Tits, their favorite female counselor, under his towel and put it in the soap dish as he grabbed the conditioner.

"You better hurry up and bail before I start," Seth had said. "Or you're going to have to watch." The guy didn't even care if Finn saw his hard-on, and while it surprised Finn, it also had turned him on. He hadn't thought anyone but Bay would be so open, but Seth lathered his cock and went to work. He turned and caught Finn's eyes and the fact that he was hard. "Well, if you're staying, you might as well get after it." He gestured to Finn's cock, and the two stroked in time with one another. Finn tried to keep his attention on the picture of the woman, but he kept sneaking glances at Seth's stiff cock.

"Like what you see?" Seth whispered, bringing Finn back to the present.

Finn shrugged. "She's a hot woman." He wasn't going to admit he'd been peeking, wishing he could touch him.

Seth had always been bold, and his voice still grabbed Finn's attention. "I'm up for some fun, too. You want to pair up?"

Finn glanced at Raven who seemed all for it. She and Kari were already eying one another. "Yeah."

But just as they were about to walk down the long hall and find a private room, Finn heard his name.

Bay stood a few feet away with his wife Lila, who was looking incredible in her skintight white dress that was nothing more than a scrap of fabric carefully placed to hide all the naughty parts. Her diamond collar sparkled around her neck, and she smiled at Finn as his eyes lingered a little too long.

"Looks like you two were going to start all the fun without me." Bay held out his hand to Seth, and the two shook so tight, Finn wondered if their pissing match would ever end. Bay didn't seem to like the way Seth was eying Lila.

"We were," Seth said. "Would you like to join us? We came looking for a threesome, but we're always down for more."

Bay nodded. "Let's go to my private suite, and we'll get this party started."

Bay led the way, and Finn's heart sank. He hoped he was going to set something up, but with Bay around, Seth would never agree to it.

"Lila is going to watch," Bay said. "She's been a bad girl."

"Yes, sir," she said. Her eyes were ringed red and getting worse by the minute, and soon after, tears were flowing.

As soon as they were in the private suite, Finn wasted no time taking out his cock and Bay followed, along with Seth. The other two women dropped to their knees and began servicing. Raven worked Seth, and his young bride started off licking Finn's cock from base to tip and then took a turn on Bay's.

They knew better than to even look at Lila, who was no doubt going to be dripping wet by the time Bay allowed anyone to touch her. Finn had always thought the woman was gorgeous, but he turned his head and met Bay's eyes.

"Do you like what you see?" Bay asked.

Finn didn't know if Bay meant him or Lila, but the answer was the same either way. "Yes."

"Then take her." Bay put his hand on Kari's head and held her on his cock. He was buried good and deep in her throat, and she was puffing hard, gasping for air as Finn turned away.

He looked over to see Raven tugging Seth's balls, twisting them as he commanded, and she loved it. It was hot to see her really get into it, and she looked over and blew him a kiss before he approached Lila.

Bay thrusted like a wild man, and Kari pulled away gagging and choking. "Don't be fucking gentle with her," Bay growled to Finn.

Seth turned his head and finally got a look at how Bay was deepthroating his girl. "Give her all you got; she's used to it."

"Don't worry. I plan on it."

Finn felt kind of sorry for the girl because he knew that Bay was being rough on purpose, not only to upset his wife but to show Seth that he was top dog.

As soon as Finn approached Lila, she dropped to her knees and got on his cock. She was so hungry for attention and eager to please, he knew that she had something to prove.

After they'd gotten more comfortable, Bay released Kari so she could go be with Seth, who was balls deep inside Raven.

Bay swatted Lila's ass. "Stand up."

"Yes, sir." She got to her feet but leaned over, still sucking Finn's cock. "That's a good girl." He leaned over and regarded Finn. "Take her from the front. I'm going to fuck her ass."

Lila moaned and stood up, kissing Finn as she lifted her leg and stuck out her hips for him to bury his cock deep inside.

Seth took his ladies and went across the room where he lined them up and bent them over. Bay stepped forward and rubbed his cock all over Lila's ass, and even Finn's balls. The music in the club was so loud that one might barely hear a safe word, but it was okay because this group didn't have one. Finn thrust harder, knowing he needed to feel that cock against him, and that was when Bay leaned forward, well taller than Lila and whispered in Finn's ear.

"Is this what you've been wanting?" His voice was low and breathy, and Finn's cock hardened inside Lila even more.

"Close enough." He met Bay's eyes, and Bay glanced over at Seth, who couldn't even see them from his angle on the platform he was using.

"What would you do for more?" Bay's hand stroked his hip, sending waves of electricity through his whole body.

"Anything you ask of me." He would do anything for him, or *with* him. All he had to do was ask. He'd been waiting for him to ask for years.

Bay's hand went up and down his hip, stroking his hot flesh as he pumped his cock in and out of Lila. He could feel Bay's cock enter her, too, and it was even hotter knowing they were stroking each other through her thin membrane. "I want you to hook up with Seth.

I need dirt before he leaves town. Get me something foul on camera, and I'll reward you."

"Why do you need *me*?" Finn asked.

"If you're not interested, I'll handle it myself, but he's always popping into town and not letting me know when. I'm never ready for him. You could offer some more fun before they leave. Don't tell me you weren't eying his big fat head."

Bay's voice was sending chills down his back, and Finn could feel his load about to pop. "I'm so fucking close."

"Fill her up like she was your own." Bay reached down and gripped Finn's heavy sac as he unloaded it, still buried deep.

"Tell him the good news, darling," Bay whispered in her ear.

Lila turned her head up, her eyes filled with tears. "I'm pregnant."

"Congratulations," Finn said, unsure what to think. Jealousy burned in his heart. Bay was even more unattainable now.

"What do you say, Lila?" Bay asked.

"Thank you."

Bay continued to pound her, and Finn wasn't about to pull out, not when he was this close to Bay. All he had to do was imagine that Lila wasn't between them. Bay's mouth was close enough to kiss, and Finn closed his eyes a few times, hoping he'd take the hint. He moved inside Lila and was hard again before he knew it.

"Lay down so Lila can ride you." Bay's voice was commanding and such a turn on.

They moved up to the nearest platform, and as Finn laid back, Lila climbed on top, facing him and presenting her ass to her husband. Bay pushed into her ass, and Finn felt his balls slapping against his. It didn't take him nearly as long to finish this time, especially when Bay announced his release and pulled out to pour all over Finn's sac.

Bay moved beside him to lay down as Lila rode Finn for all he was worth, panting and moaning, her walls gripping him tight as she soaked his cock.

"Do this for me, and I'll not only let you have what you crave, but I'll finance the movie."

"Okay, I'll try. I can't promise you anything." He didn't know how he was going to pull off Bay's request.

"I've got the equipment; I just need you to get the evidence. Set it up tonight and let me know as soon as possible."

Finn turned his eyes to Lila, who didn't seem too impressed with the idea. He wondered if she would run her mouth.

Bay must have realized what he was thinking. "Don't worry, Finn. My sweet Lila doesn't open her fucking mouth unless I say so, do you darling?" He pulled up his pants and did his zipper.

"No, sir." She shook her head and focused on her pleasure, which she seemed to enjoy.

"I'll do it," Finn said. "You promise?"

"Don't insult me, Finn. I gave you my word. But in case it's not enough," he gave Finn a quick peck on the mouth, "does that seal it?"

"Yes." He wasn't sure he liked having to make a deal to get his way with Bay, but if that was what it took, he was down. This might be his only chance.

Bay moved closer to his ear. "Good, get me that fucking tape." He rose up and took Lila's hand to help her down from the platform. She righted her dress and Bay rubbed her tummy. "See, darling? You did just fine."

"Thank you. May we, please go home now?" She didn't seem to be able to look the other three in the eyes, and Finn wondered if Bay was going to make her stay and perform for Seth.

"Very well, let's go." Bay led her out, and Finn made his way over to the rest of the group at the other side of the private room.

Seth was lying back with his thick cock in his hand while Kari sucked his balls and Raven serviced Kari with her long fingers.

"They had to leave?" Raven asked, sounding disappointed. She always liked to taste everyone in the room.

Finn nodded. "Yes, Lila was tired."

"I'm afraid we're not too far behind them," Seth said. "Which is such a shame. I was hoping that Kari and you would get to play a little bit. I've told her about the past a little. She loves to get off to our shower stories."

The ladies sat up, and Kari wiped her lips which were spread into a smile.

"Does she?" Finn asked. "Well, I was hoping that maybe we could hook up again before you cut out of town." Finn knew if he wanted Bay, he'd have to make it happen.

"Yeah, we're not staying long, but I know we'll have time tomorrow evening sometime. It might be a bit spur of the moment if that's okay?"

Finn passed him his card. "Hit me up. I'll make time." Raven took his hand, and he helped her to her feet as she gathered her clothes.

Seth and Kari left shortly after, leaving him and Raven to walk out alone.

"I hope you had fun," Finn said. He hadn't expected the night to go that way.

"It was amazing. We'll hook up again before you leave town?" She looked up at him with hopeful eyes.

"Yes, I promise." He just had one thing to do first. He couldn't believe the lengths he'd go to for that man.

4

DAREK

Darek rolled over and felt the warm body of someone next to him. He opened his eyes and realized that Lizzy had fallen asleep, too, and the movie they'd found on cable was long over. He glanced at the clock and couldn't believe it was just midnight. It felt like he'd been asleep for hours, more than the two since he'd crashed.

Lizzy had been in a bad mood for at least an hour after the encounter with the manager at what was now Gas and Guzzle. When they go to their reserved room, they unloaded their stuff and settled in to discuss what had happened.

She was most upset about the fire at Camp V and that no one had even told her about it. Even though Darek wanted the trip to fail, he felt horrible for her.

It was hard to live this lie, but it was all he could do. He had to do his job, he had to protect her, and most of all, he had to support her while steering her away from anything concrete that would reveal his secret connection to the camp. The more he thought about it, the more it seemed like someone had already taken care of the evidence by burning down the Camp, but he would find out more about that in the morning.

He moved closer to Lizzy, knowing he should be a gentleman and get the fuck up and move to the other bed, but he didn't want to. He was content to hold her for a moment and pretend he was someone else with a different life.

She stirred a little and then sat straight up in the bed. "Shit, did I fall asleep?"

"We both did." He sat up and grabbed his pillow. "I should go to my own bed."

"Only if you want to."

He knew things couldn't get too heated with the fucking brand on his shoulder, but then she leaned over and turned off the lamp.

"Are you sure?" The last time they got this close, they nearly let things go too far, but she nodded.

She rested on her side. "It's not like we can't control ourselves, and besides, we've already slept this long together. Why move now? Housekeeping will thank you."

"Fine, but I can't promise I'll stay on my own side." Darek planned on lying as close as possible, and he wasn't going to apologize if his hard-on offended her.

"You're good. Trust me. I think it would be nice to have someone hold me. I haven't spooned much since my divorce." She blushed, and he reached up and pushed a stray hair behind her ear.

"I didn't spoon much since I got married."

"Your ex sounds like an ice-cold bitch." She covered her mouth and smiled. "Sorry, I guess I shouldn't say everything I think."

"Yeah, that sums it up." He laughed and rolled over on his back to stare at the ceiling. "And don't worry about it. You're absolutely right. She's an ice queen."

"At least she didn't fight you in the end and gave you your house back." Lizzy fluffed her pillow and eased closer.

"It's the only decent thing she's done."

"Was that really true about the kissing?" Lizzy asked. "Or were you just kidding around?"

"Sadly, it was true. I thought I'd forgotten how for a while there." It was the truth, and he remembered months and months where he hadn't gotten more than a peck on the lips or cheeks. No deep kisses, no making out, and only a few small pecks when he left for work. A person would give a pet more fucking affection.

"I don't understand it," Lizzy said. "You're really sexy and a great kisser. Is she mentally unstable?"

"You think I'm sexy?" He turned his head toward her, and she giggled in a way he'd never heard before. She sounded ten years younger and was suddenly acting bashful. "Since when do you blush?"

He turned his body to face her, lying on his right side in case she wanted to make out, his branded shoulder would get far less attention.

"Am I?" she asked. "I guess you do that to me. Or maybe because it's been a while. My ex was like an overgrown child at times, and it was hard to get him to show me affection, too. He just wanted to get down to business, so to speak."

Darek only wished he had that problem. He couldn't even let Lizzy see him with his shirt off, but maybe taking it slow was the way to her heart. "I'd want to savor every minute."

She moved closer. "Would you?"

"Yeah, at the right time. I mean, we *are* partners. Coworkers. You're my superior, so to speak. Things could get complicated, you know? Then comes regrets."

She let out a sigh as he ticked off the reasons they shouldn't. "You sound like you don't really want to."

Darek reached out and rested his arm on her hip, and then he leaned forward to kiss her. The kiss was deep and lingering, languid and sultry. She moved her hips forward and hitched her leg up over his. The two fell comfortably against one another as if that was the way they were meant to be, and when he pulled away, he looked into her eyes. "Do you still think I don't want to?"

"Then what's keeping you?"

"Maybe I think good things come to those who wait." He shrugged.

"Do you?"

"Yeah, I think what we have is worth more, and I want to make sure it's the right time so I don't lose you. I don't want any room for regret. Besides, you putting in a word for me might go a little further if we're not sleeping together."

She laughed and rolled away from him. "I should have known. Are you worried about your promotion? Well, at least that makes sense." She sat up and grabbed her fluffy pillow, but he took her arm and pulled her down to his chest.

"Don't go anywhere. I'm just being honest. I want you, Lizzy. More than anyone ever."

"Then prove it," she said.

"Lay down and I will." He was hard as a rock for her, and as she moved back against him, he knew there was no way she didn't feel his hard length pressing against her ass. But just in case she missed it, he pressed it against her and heard her breath hitch. "Does that prove it to you?"

She moved her ass against him and moaned. "Yes."

She gave a little cry as he nuzzled his nose against her neck and breathed warm air that gave her chills. He felt them rise on her arms, and he reached up to cup her breasts. Soon, his hand was down the front of her panties, his fingers searching for her clit.

When he found it, he pressed hard, and she moved between his fingers and his thick cock. She came, and he pulled his fingers free and, with a moan, licked them clean.

"Let me help you." She reached back and took his cock into her grip and rubbed him up and down her ass, her hand jerking him in a steady rhythm that had him on the edge of orgasm before he knew it.

"I'm close."

"Come for me, Darek." She met his eyes. Suddenly, her grip tightened, and his load splashed her hand.

She brought a taste to her lips, and he thought he was going to pass out he was so lightheaded. She was overwhelming, and he couldn't believe the two of them were so hot for each other. The irony was almost too much for him, and as much as he wanted to be closer to her, he couldn't blow his cover.

"I need to wash my hands, but I'll bring back a towel." She got up and went to the bathroom. While she was gone, he wasn't sure what to fucking think about what just happened. So much for being careful and not throwing caution to the wind. He knew that any act of intimacy was only going to make things harder for him, but he couldn't help but be head over heels for Lizzy.

She came back to the bed, and once he cleaned up and righted his shorts, they curled up together.

"Maybe we should get a little practice spooning," she said with laughter in her voice.

"I'm all for that." He pulled her closer.

"I'm anxious for tomorrow. Isn't it exciting that we'll get to go to the camp?" She reminded him of a kid on Christmas Eve, with a gleam in her eyes and the hope for the morning to come.

"Yeah, I can't wait. I always wanted to go to summer camp when I was a kid." Darek didn't find it exciting in the same way she did. The kind of excitement he had was going to give him an ulcer if he wasn't careful. If he didn't have one already.

His job was high stress enough without all of this, but at least he could try and do some good to help the other guys, who were not only targets now but who had moved on with their lives and repented in their own ways. He wasn't sure that they weren't about to blow the lid off the Zodiacs and the fact that he was a part of the group, but he knew he had to make arrangements to disassociate himself from them as soon as possible. The first thing he was going to do when he got back home was figure out how to do it. There had to be a way to get rid of the mark, even if he had to take matters into his own hands.

5

FINN

He hadn't intended on waking up with Raven in his arms, but the excitement from the night before had given them a change of plans. After they shared a shower, she dressed and smelled up his bathroom with the fruitiest smelling perfume ever, and he stood at the window thinking of the task ahead.

He had always known that Seth and Bay were in a constant tug of war with one another, and even though Bay had always been the clear leader of the Zodiacs, Seth was always there to challenge him. Ever since the club had formed, the two had been posturing, and Finn often wondered why Bay allowed the other guy to be in his club at all. Maybe Bay couldn't find another Aries.

Raven walked over to the window and gave him a kiss on the cheek. "I'll see you later, lover. Call me if you need anything."

"Thanks, Raven." He gave her hand a squeeze. She'd been so good to him since he'd arrived in town, and if it weren't for her, he'd have been lost. "You know I will."

With one last smile, she shut the door behind her as she left. He brushed his hand through his damp hair and raked it back. The one unruly strand fell back into his eyes, and he left it, knowing putting up a fight with it was no use. It had always won. He decided he might as well dress and get ready for his day, but his phone rang while he dug through his suitcase for a clean pair of jeans.

The number on the screen wasn't familiar, but he had a feeling he knew who it was. "Hello?" He held his breath and hoped he was right.

"Finn? It's Seth."

"Hey, man. I thought it might be you. Don't tell me you're ready for me now?" He gave a sultry laugh and hoped the man wasn't calling to cancel.

"Actually, I was thinking tomorrow around five or six? I know it's kind of early in the evening, but we have a late flight home, and I thought it would be nice to see you. Maybe you could give Kari and me a nice send off."

"I'd like that." He knew Bay would like it, too, and it meant that before he went, he'd have to go over to Bay's and get the equipment.

"So, tell me, Finn, do you still work that mouth of yours like you used to?"

Finn didn't hook up with many men intentionally, but occasionally, things in sex club orgies got a little passionate, and he'd found himself in the position. He'd always thought of Bay during those times, just like when he and Seth had been together in the shower at camp.

"I can sure as hell try if that's what you want," Finn said. Knowing Seth was down for exactly what Bay wanted to see had him turned on.

"You know I always liked it, and I think it's something Kari would appreciate. She's turned on when I top another man."

"Then consider me your bottom." Finn felt his cock twitch as his adrenaline pumped.

"Perfect. It's so hard to find someone who is discreet. I know I can count on you for that." He seemed confident, and Finn knew that being a fellow Zodiac, sharing the same secret, was what had built that trust.

"Of course," Finn said. "You know, I'm surprised you came to town with all of this shit going on with the murders. You heard about Logan, right?"

"Logan? No, I read about Tad in the papers. Poor guy. His uncle really did a number on him, didn't he? Do you think he just snapped or what?"

"You're really that far out of the loop?" Finn wondered how Seth could not know what was going on, but then, it had all just gone down. "There's someone in New York slicing up Zodiacs and the people they love. I'm on my way out of town as soon as possible, too. Most likely Sunday. I just have shit to do for work, and then I'm bailing. So far, they got Tad, his sister, Logan's old lady, and I don't know, like three or four others; and get this, Darek Blake is the investigator. Logan is on his way to the pen. You couldn't have picked a worse time to come for a visit. But who am I to talk."

"I doubt it's as serious as all that," Seth said. "Sounds like Logan was wrapped up in it with Tad or something worse. Bay would have called me, unless he's the one killing us off. Maybe he's in need of a new hobby." Seth's laughter sent chills down Finn's spine.

"You think it could be Bay?"

"Who else do you know that's as sadistic as that bastard? I'll keep my distance, and if anyone comes for me, they best be prepared. In Dallas, we carry guns, and we know how to use them. If this killer comes at me, he better not bring a knife to a gun fight."

Finn knew it was just like Seth to feel invincible because no other Zodiac had an ego that compared to Bay's as much as him.

"Well, I hope you *do* shoot them. It would appear that you and I are next."

"What the hell do you mean?" Seth asked.

"If this fucker is going in order, it's me next and then you. It's just a theory, but Bay thinks we're safe as long as Logan's kicking around in prison."

"That's the dumbest thing I've ever heard of, and how does Bay know so much? Again, if someone is murdering Zodiacs, it's him. And he can come at me all day; I'm not afraid of him." He laughed like it was the most ridiculous thing in the world, and Finn wished he was as confident. "Think about what you're saying, Finn. You just said that someone is killing Zodiacs, but that's not true. Tad jumped out of a fucking window, and Logan is in jail. He's not dead. Out of all the killings, not one of them has been a Zodiac."

"Tad might have had help going out that window, and Logan's girlfriend was nearly cut in half, Seth. Could you imagine if that were Kari? Either way, we're the targets, and someone is making us suffer."

"I think Logan got himself mixed up in something and Tad threw himself out that window for the guilt over killing his uncle. Case solved. Darek's work should be a piece of cake." He gave another laugh, and Finn knew there was no convincing the guy. He focused on the task and how he and Bay were going to set it up.

"Maybe you're right. I'll see you later?"

"Yeah, I'll let Kari know we have a big send-off. See you then."

The phone went dead, and Finn thought about what he'd learned. He couldn't ignore that things were happening with Zodiacs, but maybe it wasn't what it seemed.

He had to go to Bay's to get the equipment and decided to make arrangements. Knowing Bay hated getting calls from out of nowhere, he decided to text. Bay sent a one-word response. *Penthouse.*

On his way to the penthouse, he thought about telling Bay Seth's theory to see his reaction. He didn't think that Bay was targeting him, but maybe he'd know more information that could help. He wondered just how much he didn't know, considering Seth was in the dark. He also wondered why Seth hadn't been contacted. Shouldn't they let the others in on what was going on? Had Bay, as their leader, been in touch? Finn hadn't gotten a formal call, but then again, he'd come to town to do his business with Bay.

He arrived at the penthouse where Bay conducted all of his business, and he wondered if he'd have to submit to a strip search as usual.

He knocked on the door and was surprised when a younger woman answered. "Come in." She stepped aside and held the door open for him. The girl looked very much like a younger version of Bay's wife Lila, and he couldn't help but wonder if she was related. She was also wearing a very short French maid's costume and holding a white dust rag.

Finn entered and joined Bay in the front room. "I see you're cloning women now."

"Yes, Mia is my sister-in-law. She's repaying a debt today by cleaning the place for me. I didn't think you'd mind her being here."

The young woman walked over to the coffee table and bent over to wipe it. Her ass stuck out, and Finn could see everything she had. His pulse quickened at the sight of her.

"No, of course not." He didn't see any reason for her to be there, other than to get under his skin, but Finn didn't let any emotion show on his face.

"Mia, do me a favor and check Mr. Wheeler for wires."

"Yes, sir," she said.

As she smiled and walked over, Finn realized why she was there. Bay knew how to put people on edge. She ran her hands up his chest and down his arms. Then she reached around behind him and felt his back. Her hands moved lower, grazing his hard cock and cupping his balls.

He turned his head and whispered in her ear. "They're nice and full."

"Indeed." She smiled, and Bay cleared his throat. She turned around and looked him in the eye. "He's clean."

"Thank you. Now get back to work." Bay sipped his drink and put his feet on the coffee table. "I'd offer her to you, but I don't share her."

Finn took the chair beside him. "I'm good. I'm meeting Seth between five and six tomorrow for a little send-off. I actually had an interesting conversation with him and was shocked at how uninformed he was about a certain situation going on with our friends." He hated having to be careful, but with Mia around, he had no choice.

Bay shrugged. "It's not my fucking job to keep them informed. You guys act like I'm your fucking babysitter."

"He's a potential target, Bay. Don't you think that a little heads up is fair?" He knew that Bay didn't care much for Seth, but to let him be in danger and say nothing? That was low, even for Bay Collins.

"Consider yourself special."

"I'd say I'm honored, but really, Bay. Someone should explain to the rest of the guys what we're up against." It wasn't fair that they had targets on their backs and no one had told them.

"And what are we up against? Do you know? Because I don't. I can't exactly say what we're facing." He shrugged like it didn't matter.

Finn knew he'd have to take on the task himself. Once he was back home and safe, he'd do just that. "Is there anything you're not telling me? Something I could pass along?"

"Oh, now you don't trust me?" Bay narrowed his eyes. "I'm hurt, Finn. To think that you say you're in love with me, and now this? Perhaps I'm the one who shouldn't trust you."

Finn turned to see Mia across the room listening. She turned her head back toward the table she wiped and then walked to the other side of the room. Finn looked back at Bay, who was downing a drink. "That's not what I'm saying. I *do* trust you. Of course, I do. I'm here, aren't I?" He felt like a scrambling fool trying to keep Bay from being angry with him. Finn was so close to having his fantasy come true.

"Yes, because you need my money," Bay said. "Don't think that I don't know what means most to you. Your art is always going to come before anyone else, Finn. It's true, and you know it. You're not willing to get on your knees tonight for *me*. That's all for my money."

"You want me on my knees? All you have to do is say so right now. Your little friend can watch." Finn wasn't about to be intimidated. He'd had enough of the posturing.

Bay sat forward in his chair. "If you kneel, it will be to do my whim. Look around. Do you think I need your sex? I need your commitment; sex is only a reward." He turned to the girl and held out his hand. "Come to me, Mia."

Mia walked over and took his hand. Then Bay pulled her down into his lap. He stroked her hair like she was his pet. "Mia, tell Finn why you're being punished."

"I took money from Bay's wallet to buy coke."

"And what had I told you?"

"To come to you when I needed a fix," she said.

Bay nodded. "And you didn't. Why?"

"Because you had told me no when I asked."

Bay reached over to the table beside him and opened a wooden box. Then he took out a small packet of cocaine and tossed it on the table. "You see? She didn't trust that I would provide if she gave herself to me. Instead, she stole, and she ended up buying some shit that made her sick."

The girl began to cry, and Bay pushed her off his lap. "Go ahead. Have it."

Mia turned and looked at the bag, but she didn't touch it until she looked back at Bay. Like a whipped dog, she'd learned her lesson.

Bay met Finn's eyes. "Who loves you, Mia?"

She hugged his knee. "You do, Bay." Mia caressed his thigh and then rubbed his cock through his pants.

"Can I get the camera?" Finn was growing bored and a bit jealous of Bay's display.

"Yes, of course. Mia, go get the package from the bar."

She moaned a little in protest as if she didn't want to leave his side, and Finn couldn't blame her. For Bay Collins to give him that same attention was something he'd fantasized about for years.

He wanted to be just as important and trusted. Maybe this task was his first test.

Mia walked across the room and came back with the envelope. Bay pulled her into his lap and kissed her shoulder as she passed Finn the package.

"It's in this?" Finn asked.

"Yes, it's really easy. There is an app for your phone. You make sure it's set to record, and you leave it somewhere that it can see what you're doing. I want something salacious."

"I think I can manage."

"See that you do. And Finn, I really hope you took something from Mia's lesson."

Finn thought about it as he left and realized he had. Trusting Bay was the only way.

6

DAREK

Lizzy had been in a strange mood all morning, and there was no indication that she and Darek had been intimate in any way the night before. He didn't know if she was trying hard to prove that she wasn't going to let her feelings get in the way of her job, but she was ready to go to work before he opened his eyes and had even gotten him breakfast for the road and offered to drive.

She sat behind the wheel, taking them to Camp Victory. "I'm going to have to get this car cleaned inside and out when we get back to the city."

"I'm trying not to make a mess." Darek shoved the last bite of his breakfast sandwich into his mouth. The thing had been made up of two pancakes, an egg, and the thinnest bacon he'd had in years. "Thanks again for getting it for me."

"Yeah, well, the hotel had a good spread. It seemed terrible to let it all go to waste, and I thought you'd need your rest for the day. I know this is going to be boring for you, and I didn't want you falling asleep on me." She gave him a wink as she slowed the car and took the next road, which led to the camp.

Darek's stomach tied in knots. "Bored? Why do you think that?"

"I know you didn't want to come on this trip and that you think this is a waste of time, which you might just be right about if the fire really *did* destroy the main office."

He brushed the crumbs off of his pants. "We're about to see."

"Yeah, I think this place is close." She narrowed her eyes at him, but he pointed ahead.

"See, I was right. We're here." He had to remember not to seem too familiar with the camp, and he was thankful he was much different now than he'd been as a kid.

She turned and looked at the big sign overhead. "It's actually a nice place."

Darek took one look and knew it had been remodeled since he'd last been around. Sure enough, where the log cabin used to be, a large metal and stone building stood in its place. They'd rebuilt it not to burn, and he breathed a sigh of relief as she pulled up and parked in the new rock lot.

"Well, it looks like a new structure," Lizzy said. "Let's hope it's just been remodeled and not replaced." Lizzy's mouth was turned down in a frown, and Darek reached over and took her hand.

"Hey, stay positive." He winked, and she stared right through him. He realized that she was looking over his shoulder.

"Can I help you?" A voice called out from behind him, and he turned to see a man in khaki shorts walking over.

Lizzy opened her door and so did Darek. While she walked around the car to join the men, the old man held out his hand to Darek. "I'm the owner, Greg Williford."

"I'm Detective Blake. This is Special Agent McNamara with the FBI. We're here working on an old case."

Greg's expression turned serious. "Oh? You mean the Johnson case? That girl who got murdered over a decade ago?"

Lizzy stepped up and offered her hand, which the man promptly shook. "Yes, sir. We have reason to believe the killer was falsely identified and that maybe one of the boys from Camp Victory had something to do with it."

The news shocked the man, who covered his mouth and rubbed

his stubbly chin. "I can't imagine any of our boys doing that. Most come back year after year."

"Which is why we'd like to look at the registration lists from back then." She had a hopeful look in her eyes, and Darek watched her hope fade as Mr. Williford shook his head.

"I'm afraid that's not possible. We had a fire out here a few years back, and it destroyed all of our old paperwork. All we had was what was left here by the original owners. When we took over just two years before the fire, we started keeping electronic records. Those were recovered by our system, but the paper files hadn't been transferred."

Lizzy frowned. "So, you're telling me that there's no record of who attended back then. Is there someone we can ask? Someone who would remember names from that year?"

Darek knew that was a stretch and hoped he wasn't about to take a walk down memory lane that could get him identified. He'd gotten lucky so far.

"Not that I know of. The place had been shut down for a year before we showed up to buy it, so everyone that worked for the other owners had scattered to the winds. We started fresh here, my wife and me."

"I see. Well, it's a beautiful place." Lizzy looked around, and Darek could tell that the grounds were used recently. Banners still hung, and the kids' art was on display on the front door of the main office.

"Thank you," Greg said. "The kids just left yesterday, so it's a bit of a mess, but you're welcome to take a look around. Some of the cabins were burned that were close to the main office and the mess hall, but many of the structures, the playground, and the activities center are still the same."

"I know this might sound like a dumb question, but have you ever seen symbols painted anywhere?" She reached into her pocket and pulled out a list of the zodiac symbols.

"Oh no. I heard about that." Greg shook his head. "My wife was in town, and someone told her all about the zodiac symbols. They said the killer had carved them into that poor girl's back. I didn't think it was true. I told her not to listen to gossip. Us being new around here, they were saying lots of things to scare us off."

"Scare you off?" Darek thought that was a little odd. Who would want to do that?

The older man scratched his head. "Yeah, well, I don't know who it was, but I kept getting some threats about opening the camp back up. I figured it was some of the locals who'd either attended or who liked the other owners better. I didn't listen to them. I didn't even tell the police about it until the fire, but by then, of course, it was too late to find out who did it."

Lizzy closed the distance between them and placed her hand on the man's shoulder. "What kind of threats were they? Phone calls?"

"No, they left notes. I didn't bother to keep them." He gave them an apologetic look.

Darek was glad the notes no longer existed, but he wished he'd gotten a look at them. Bay was capable of making threats like that, and he was also Darek's biggest suspect in the burning of the main office. He wondered if Bay would admit it. He sure didn't seem worried about the two of them going on this little adventure. Maybe that was why?

Darek couldn't let Lizzy ask all the questions. "Did the notes have those symbols on them?"

The old man met Darek's eyes and held up his hands. "No, and I've never seen them before. I wish I could help."

Lizzy patted his arm. "You've been very helpful. We'll just go look around if that's okay."

"Feel free. It's a big place. You can take my cart if you like." Mr. Williford dug into his pocket, but Lizzy backed away.

"No thank you. On a beautiful day like this, we'll walk." She turned to Darek, and he wished that she'd have just taken the damned cart. She had no idea how fucking big the place was, and even though it was a nice sunny day, it was also going to be heating up soon, and he didn't want to work any harder than he had to.

The two walked away from the office and headed out on the path that led toward the activities center, or where Darek remembered it being anyway.

The sun was beating down on his forehead, and he wiped his brow. "We should have taken him up on the ride."

"And miss out on a walk with you? I don't think so." She gave him an elbow, and then her face lit up with a smile that told him she *did* remember the night before and it hadn't been a dream. He was beginning to think she'd wanted to forget about it.

Being in the camp was strange, and he tried not to focus too hard on the past for fear that something he'd blocked out might come creeping up on him. He didn't pay attention to the shower house or look out to the dock where they used to go fishing for hours on end, and he damned sure didn't want to look toward his old cabin or the cabins where the counselors stayed. He kept his head down and thought about what a beautiful walk down memory lane this could be for a normal person, someone who never met Bay Collins or joined the Zodiacs and felt an emptiness inside him.

They walked to the water and Lizzy paused, looking down to where the old millhouse was. "What's that?"

He looked up, and before he could stop her, she took off. "Wait," he called out. "It's just some old storage or wellhouse probably. You need to watch for snakes." He took off and caught up to her. "Slow down."

"It could be a hideout. Some place these little shits go to sneak away from supervision."

And here he thought they'd been original. There were enough trees and brush to hide the place from the camp, and only someone like Lizzy would even notice it. Then again, she was a detective, and this was her job.

"I just think it's a waste to run all the way out there." His heart was beating, the sweat beading on his brow, and when they made it to the patch of trees that separated the old mill site from camp, he froze.

"Think about it, Darek. If you were some twisted little fucker stuck at camp goody-two-shoes all summer, you'd want a secret place, right?" She walked over toward the entrance, and Darek's vision went blurry.

He felt the ground beneath him as he hit it hard, landing in the tall weeds.

"Darek!" Lizzy's voice sounded like she was at the other end of a tunnel, and when he opened his eyes, he couldn't see anything but the earth. She rolled him over and wiped his brow. "Are you okay?"

"Yes, I guess I just got too hot or something." He hadn't wanted to tell her about his condition and have her think he was batshit crazy, especially since she'd already put in a good word for him at the FBI.

She offered him a hand, and he got to his feet and dusted himself off, but he couldn't stop itching. There were all kinds of plants in the little patch he'd fallen in, but he didn't think much of it. As long as he wasn't on a snake, he was good.

"We should get you back to the hotel." Lizzy brushed him off, and he stepped away, standing on his own.

"I'm fine." He didn't want her to fuss over him.

"Are you sure?" He nodded, and she stepped away to the old structure, which was in much worse shape now than it had been years ago. "Good, I wanted to check out the building."

"It looks like a perfect place to get a snake bite," he said. He didn't want her to find the millstone where Emily had been tied. Surely, the thing was bloodstained, and the symbols had been painted around the edges.

She rolled her eyes. "I'll just look in the doorway; I won't go inside. Please don't faint on me again. I've never seen a grown man go down like that."

He was self-conscious but let the remarks go. He just hoped she didn't look at him any differently. The last thing he needed was to feel weak.

He walked with her up to the doorway, carefully watching their steps in case she didn't, and hoping the stone had been covered in grass or dirt that had washed in from a high river.

"Damn, look at that big stone," she said.

Darek's adrenaline started pumping as he turned his head to see the millstone, but it was nothing like he expected. The thing was dirty and covered in mud, and he could tell that the paintings were gone. The thing had been flipped over.

"That thing has to weigh a ton," he said. He couldn't help but wonder who had managed to turn it over, and once again, Bay popped into his mind. The man had thought of everything.

7

BAY

Bay could think of a hundred better ways to end his workweek than to meet with Logan Miller, but with the man about to transfer to much harsher conditions, he needed him to be aware of what he was walking into.

Logan was sitting on the other side of the table with his hands cuffed in front of him. He looked pretty good, considering the shitty food they'd been feeding him and his terrible sleeping conditions.

"I never thought I'd be so glad to see you," Logan said as he held out his hand, his cuffs rattling as Bay shook his hand.

Bay lowered himself into the chair and then took out some papers to look busy. "I wanted to let you know that they've arranged your transfer. Your trial is set for a couple of months, and that was the best I could do."

Logan shrugged. "It's okay, man. I'm good in here."

Bay hated his false sense of security. He saw it not only as a sign of weakness but as a sign of stupidity. "I don't think you understand what a shithole you're about to enter."

"One where the killer can't reach me. That's where. You guys are sitting ducks. Even if I get my ass beat, I'm still better off." He smiled like an idiot, and Bay wasn't sure he hadn't snapped. Too bad it was too late for a plea of insanity.

"You're delusional if you think an ass beating is all you're up against. There are gangs, men who will make you their woman, and others who will knock your teeth out so you can't bite their dicks while you're blowing them. The others are just going to rape your ass, and you'll be lucky if you spend much time sitting down."

"You're just trying to scare me," Logan said. "I know it's bad, but I plan on keeping to myself."

Bay shook his head. "You'll do what they want you to do. *Who* they want you to do. You're nothing in there. Don't forget it."

Logan's eyes darkened, and finally, the look of fear crossed his face that Bay was looking for.

"Now, fear not, for I've come to bring hope." Bay used a dramatic voice, but only he was humored by it. "Your stay on the inside can be horrible or tolerable, but that's all up to you and how much you decide to talk. I'm sure you get where I'm coming from, don't you? After all, I'm the one who pulls the strings, so you'll do things my way."

Logan looked down at his cuffs and gave a slight nod.

"Good," Bay said. "I'll make sure that you're taken care of once you get there, a mercy that I'm prepared to extend you for as long as you're willing to play by my rules."

"I understand."

"Good. Because it's that easy. I'll look after you if you look after me."

"Have you heard anything about Hannah? Did they find her?"

"No, no word, but don't worry. I'm sure she's fine. Probably living it up somewhere and thinking about the bullet she dodged when you were arrested."

Logan's lip curled, and if he had fangs, he'd have bared them. "How can you talk about her like that? She could be dead somewhere because of us, and you're here making jokes." He slapped the table. "She's not like that."

"I hate to break it to you, but I know her better than you think,

Logan." Bay gave him a smug look, and Logan's eyes burned with anger.

"You're a fucking liar. She hated you."

Bay nodded. "Only because I didn't call her after we fucked. Tell me, how's that little apple-shaped birthmark on her hip? Is it just as sweet when you bite it as it used to be? I bet it is."

"Fuck you," Logan growled.

"Now, Logan, let's not fight over a woman. That was a long time ago, and I'm sure she had her reasons for not telling you. Oh, and that reminds me, is there anyone you don't want on your visitor's list? I can make arrangements."

Logan looked down at the table, his nostrils still flaring. "Aside from you?" He scratched his head. "My mother."

"Aww, you don't want her to see you this way?"

"I don't care about her, and *I* don't want to see *her*."

"Fine." Bay wondered if the woman even knew her baby boy was incarcerated. "I guess that's all for today. Make sure you do your part, and I'll do mine. Are we good?"

"Yeah, I hear you loud and clear. Do me a favor and send Katherine Fallwell in your place." Bay laughed as the guard came in and took Logan's arm.

He left the meeting room and then walked down the corridor and past security. Once he was halfway to his car, his phone buzzed, and he smiled when he saw who it was.

Bay answered the call. "How's the trip? Finding any clues?"

"You asshole," Darek cursed. "You knew it was a dead end, and you didn't give me a fucking heads up?"

"I don't know what you mean." He chuckled and then opened his car door and slid into the leather seat.

"Fuck you. The main building at camp burned down. The mill-stone was turned over and cleaned. You covered our tracks."

"Someone has to take care things," Bay said. "If it weren't for me, you'd be cuffed and stuffed by now, and I'd be visiting you in jail and not Logan fucking Miller."

"Have you been to see him again?"

"I'm just leaving," Bay said. "They arranged for his transfer, and he's still smiling like a dumbass. He really thinks he's safe in there. I had to educate him on who is calling the shots."

Darek sighed. "Please tell me you didn't threaten him. Which reminds me, did you threaten a Greg Williford about reopening the camp?"

"Never heard of him, and no. I'm not going to leave a bigger trail while trying to cover one up. Why? Did you meet with him?" He laughed and imagined how uncomfortable Darek must have been.

"Yeah, and I went out to the millhouse, too," Darek said. "How'd you manage to turn that stone over?"

"Your lack of memory is really annoying. Do you not remember how we covered your ass that night? It took every one of us to turn that fucking thing over. You helped."

"That's impossible. I'd have remembered something like that."

"Yeah, like you remember so many other important fucking things. I think I'll have your shrink give you a lower dose of your fucking meds." He knew Darek still didn't believe that he pulled his shrink's strings, too, but it was fun to make him wonder.

"I can find out if that's true, you know? And if I do, we're going to have a big fucking problem on our hands."

"What is it with you motherfuckers today?" Bay asked. "That's two threats from weak-ass men who think they can actually raise my fucking blood pressure with a couple of words." He laughed as Darek mumbled obscenities. "Save it."

"Did Logan mention Hannah?" Darek asked.

Bay wondered if Darek thought that Logan was really capable of hurting Hannah. He for one knew the guy didn't have it in him anymore.

"No, just that he was worried about her," Bay said.

"I'm afraid if she ends up dead, he's going to fucking talk."

Bay was one step ahead of him, and that was why he'd put people in place to make sure Logan didn't squeal. "Trust me; he won't. I've already told him that I hold his life in my hands. If he looks like he's going to be a threat, I'll take care of it." Bay didn't see any reason not to be honest. It wasn't like Darek would do a damned thing about it.

"Dammit, Bay. It's shit like that. It makes me wonder if you don't know where Hannah is or what happened to her. Did you shut her up, too?"

Bay's eyes narrowed. "I don't know what you mean. I'll try not to be insulted." Bay hung up the phone and thought that Darek was sometimes too good at his job. Thankfully, the asshole was in just as much trouble as he was. Bay wasn't answering questions about Hannah, and if there was one thing he knew for sure, that bitch wasn't going to talk to anyone anytime soon.

8

FINN

Finn walked out of the building and to his car, which was parked a block away. Another wasted hour with an uninterested investor had passed, and Finn felt like he should just pack up and go back home with his tail tucked between his legs. Not only was he having problems finding anyone interested in working on the project, but the ones who were weren't quite what he was looking for.

If he'd known that things would be this hard, he would have stayed on with the production company he worked with for two years before, content to work behind the scenes of other people's projects. But no, he had to listen to Edie. She'd been so encouraging and wanted him to come out of his creative shell a little, and now, he knew why he had stayed in one for so long.

Before her, work had been about going to a room with a couple of others and editing footage, doing special effects, and leaving the rest to others. He had been comfortable and had even been blessed to have his screenplays looked at and accepted. The first one he'd sold had given him enough money to pay for his beautiful car, which had been a shell of what he'd made it, and the second helped him secure a nice place to live. Those jobs, unlike the few acting jobs he'd had in the past, had gotten him where he wanted to be: taken seriously.

He finally got to his car, and as he opened the door, his phone rang. Edie had called three times while he'd been talking to the potential investor, and he knew she must have something important to tell him.

"Hey, baby. I'm sorry I didn't answer. I was in a meeting for the past two hours, listening to a jackass tell me how to make my fucking work better." The advice had been unsolicited, and nothing could kill a person's spirit worse than a bad critique.

"Sorry, but the studio called and they need your slot," she said. "I told them you were out of town, and they said to let you know. You're welcome to use it after the first of the year. I told her that wasn't going to work, but she just told me to pass the message to you."

He banged his hand on the steering wheel and couldn't believe his fucking luck. It was the worst ever. "They can't do this! I paid a fucking deposit for a reason! For those assholes to hold my fucking time slot."

"I'm sorry. She said she's already sent the refund, and it should be credited to your account." Edie was quiet as he took a few deep breaths and tried not to take it out on her. She was just the messenger, and he needed her help now, more than ever.

"Look, do me a favor and call around for me," he said. "I don't care who it is, but get me some time if it's available, and watch the money because I'm having a shitty time here trying to get investors."

"I'm so sorry, baby. I wish I could hold you." Her voice set his hairs on end.

He didn't need her fucking coddling. "For fuck's sake, Edie, I'm not a child. Will you just call around?"

"Yes, of course." She sounded like a kicked puppy, and he felt like shit.

"I'm sorry, baby. I'm just so aggravated. I want this to work and I'm afraid it's all falling apart. My only investor is not sure he wants to stay in, and I can't find any others. Look, I've got another meeting in half an hour. I'm going to freshen up and head that way, so don't call me, okay? I'll let you know when I'm out." He knew the only way to make anything happen was to get Bay to bankroll the fucking production, and the way to do it was to get the dirt he wanted on Seth.

"Okay, but call me as soon as you're out, and I'll let you know if I got anyone on the phone. It's going to be tough, being a Saturday, but I'll do what I can. Don't worry, baby. I love you."

"I love you too." The words were as empty as his heart, and he hated himself for saying them. He hung up the phone and sat for a minute. He questioned why he even kept her around, but then a little voice inside him reminded him why. *She's a perfect cover, that's why.*

He hit the steering wheel again. "I'm not fucking gay. I love women." He tried his hardest to think about Raven, and while he *did* enjoy her company and the way he felt inside her, his one true love would always be a certain platinum blond man who made him question everything.

Finn thought back to what Bay had said about Mia. He didn't share her. She was special to him. His chest burned with jealousy, anger, and an aching that he couldn't explain. It was a desperate longing, like wanting something he knew he could never have.

He imagined himself submitting to Bay. Taking a knee and giving himself to the man, body, mind, and soul, to do with whatever he wanted. Could he trust someone that much? He wanted to. With everything in him, he wanted to be something special to Bay, even if Finn wasn't the only person Bay loved.

Finn hadn't known the man could hold such feelings until he'd seen him with Mia. Holding him on her lap, caressing her like a cherished pet, and taking the time to teach her to be all the things he'd wanted her to be. Could Finn be that for Bay?

He didn't understand the feelings he had in him. The way his chest ached when he thought of belonging to Bay. He tried to imagine himself with the man and knew he'd never be anything more than his dirty secret.

Bay was The Slayer. The man who made other men fear, the man who decided other men's fates, and he had ultimate control and power, which was why Finn was so turned on by him.

Even though Bay might finally let him have his way, he wasn't ever going to let anyone see that side of him.

Finn wondered if that was what he needed. He'd been a private man with Edie, and even she hadn't known about his preferences. If he could have Bay, could he be content to keep things under wraps? Finn imagined him the night at the sex club, his powerful body pumping into Lila, his long cock, so big and hard, Finn could feel it rubbing next to his during the double penetration. He could handle anything as long as he had Bay's company.

He looked down, and his cock was so hard that he felt like a strong wind would make him orgasm. Thankfully, it was time to go to Seth's hotel room and do what Bay had asked. He reached over to get the little camera set up with his phone, and once it was ready, he made sure the battery was fully charged. Then he tucked it into his pocket.

His hands shook as he drove to the hotel, and he remembered only being this nervous when he was on his way to auditions, which was why he hadn't done much acting. Even though he knew he'd be putting on a show of sorts, he needed to get his composure.

He parked and went inside, hoping that Seth was still hungry for him and wondering how Kari was going to feel about it. After a few deep breaths on the elevator, he went to the door and knocked.

Seth opened the door. "Come on in. Kari is waiting." His old friend walked him to the bedroom, and there he found Kari lying in bed with her hands bound. The wild look on her face was her trying to smile behind the ball gag.

Finn took his phone and placed it on the short dresser with the little camera attached to the side, hopefully in a position to catch everything. As Seth went into the bathroom, Finn turned it on and checked its positioning. Then he turned off the ringer. "Just silencing this thing," he said to Kari. "I don't want anything to disturb our fun."

She tried smiling again, and Seth returned with his robe removed and stroking his hard cock. "I hope you're ready for this. It's been a long time for sure."

"Yes, it has. I hope I haven't lost my touch."

"Get out of those clothes and let's see." Seth laughed, and Kari moaned from the bed. "Maybe we should see what she has to say?"

"I think so. Maybe we could put her mouth to use, too?" Finn hoped she'd be a little bit more active since she was just as much a target as Seth.

Seth went over and removed her gag, and Finn wondered just how old she was. She was tiny, and her waistline barely gave way to hips. She was as smooth as a baby's bottom.

"How old is your wife?" He didn't want to disrespect Seth by addressing his woman directly. The two obviously were okay with him dominating her, so he didn't think it would be too disrespectful.

"She's twenty," Seth said. "Isn't she sweet?"

"Yes, she is. I didn't really get to see her the other night. Bay was so busy with her and all."

"Yeah, he's lucky she likes it rough, don't you, baby girl?"

"Yes," she hissed the word and writhed on the bed, her legs scissoring in anticipation.

Seth looked at him with his dark, sexy eyes. "She's raring to go, that one. I think we should show her how we did it in the old days first. Make her want it."

He reached out and rubbed Finn's hard cock. Finn did the same for him. They stood stroking one another and then Seth curled his finger to his wife. "Come closer, kitten."

"I want to share it with him." She licked her lips and then inched her way over.

Finn turned and made sure that the act was going to be on camera, and as Kari held his hand, he dropped to his knees in front of Seth. Bay was going to get exactly what he wanted, and with any luck, so was he. He closed his eyes as he kissed and licked, feeling the warm flesh and Kari's mouth as they shared the hard cock between them. He reached up, cupped Seth's heavy sac, and felt a soft hand on his own dick.

"I want both of you." Kari looked up at Seth who grinned.

"What do you think, Finn? Should we spit roast her, or DP that tight ass?"

"I'm down for anything; you name the game, I'm playing." Her hand felt so good around him that he didn't want her to let it go.

"That's what I like to hear. How about helping me out?"

Finn knew just what Seth was asking and leaned forward to oblige.

Kari leaned over and went to work on Finn, and just when he thought his jaw couldn't take any more punishment, Seth pulled free and covered both of them with his release.

While they were still covered, he dragged his wife up by the soft cord that tied her hands and pulled her off of Finn's cock, but only until he could bury himself inside of her sweet hole. She continued after Finn got to his feet. He played with her tits and then ran his fingers through her soft hair. She looked and smelled like heaven, and while Seth pounded into her, he reached across and placed his hand on Finn's shoulder then leaned in for a strong kiss.

Finn closed his eyes and thought of Bay. With footage like this, he was going to make Bay proud.

9

DAREK

"Thanks for driving again," Lizzy said as Darek took the next left as instructed.

"No problem. Things are so much easier when you have a good GPS. I remember my dad getting lost and how every trip ended up a game to see how many quarters he owed to the swear jar."

"You had a swear jar?" She chuckled and let go of a sigh as if he'd had it easy. "My old man would have needed a bottomless pit to toss his quarters in."

"Yeah? You mean your real father?"

"Yes, and slow down a bit. The driveway will sneak up on you. The house is far from the road."

He slowed the Rover and wondered if he was actually going to learn something more about her on this trip. "How old were you when you left home?"

"I was still a minor. Robert took me in, and in case you're wondering, we didn't have a swear jar at his place, either."

"No?"

"Nope, he let me say whatever I damned well pleased, but he was a gentleman. He used words like fiddle and fork instead. I used to laugh when he'd say shoe."

"Shoe?" He couldn't imagine what he'd use the word for. Darek heard the ping of the GPS, and Lizzy leaned forward in her seat.

"Here it is." She eased back as he took the turn. "Yes, shoe, not shoot, but shoe instead of saying shit, which was probably his favorite swear word because he said it a lot."

"He sounds like a nice guy."

"He was, but I'm sure he cursed when it was just the guys."

"I mean because he took you in. That had to be a big decision for both of you. Didn't you have anywhere else to go when your father died?"

Lizzy's head turned so fast; he thought her neck might snap. "He wasn't dead."

"Oh, I'm sorry. I just assumed."

She took a deep breath and then pointed to the clearing where a large house stood in the distance, like something from a southern romance.

"Wow, this place is amazing. It seems a bit out of place, though, like it belongs in Georgia or somewhere farther south." The house had the kind of porch that was made for sitting and sipping tea or mint juleps.

"His wife was from Savannah. She passed away a while before I came into the picture."

Darek stopped out front in the gravel drive, which looked like it needed a good weeding. There were flowering trees and hedges that needed trimmed. "Does anyone come and take care of the place?"

"I have a man that comes every other month. He's not due for another week." She gave Darek a wink as she opened the door and then turned to grab her keys from the ignition.

Darek got out and stretched. He hoped the house had a nice place to kick back and relax. Their day had started early, and even though they'd gone back to the camp and the crime scene, they hadn't had any luck. The landscape just wasn't the same, and he thanked the heavens for that. Lizzy *did* ask Mr. Williford if he found anyone that might know something, to please send them to her, but the man didn't seem like he was going to find anyone.

Lizzy unlocked the door and pushed it open. Then she stepped aside to let Darek go in first. He hesitated, not used to someone holding the door open for him, but went inside where it looked like something out of an old movie. Most of the furniture was covered with sheets and drops cloths, some stained with the same colored paint that matched the walls. It didn't look like anyone had been there in ages, but Lizzy wasted no time uncovering the couches and tossing the covers into the corners. The room came to life as he helped her, especially when she drew back a large curtain that opened up to reveal a large-paned glass window with a bench seat and the most amazing view of a lake in the distance.

"Wow," Darek muttered under his breath as he walked closer.

"It's breathtaking isn't it?" He wasn't even sure she'd heard him across the room, but she continued. "This was always one of my favorite places to sit and read. I'd open the windows when the weather was nice and let the breeze blow in from across the water." She seemed to have a glow about her, as if coming back home had rejuvenated her, but it made him wonder what kind of life she had back with her father and what kind of misery the old man had taken her out of.

As she stared out the window, he turned and walked around the room, looking at the books on the large shelves that lined the wall on the far side of the room and the pictures on the mantle, and he was shocked that they were all of what could only be the man's wife.

To his right in the corner, there was a small sitting area and a chessboard, but only one chair.

"Do you play chess?" she asked.

Darek looked up to see Lizzy leaning against the wall near the window and wondered how long she'd been watching him. "No, I never learned. You?"

"Yes, although Robert and I rarely sat down to play. We'd make moves and then wait to see when the other had played. He was much better than me, but I learned quick."

Darek couldn't help but notice that the game was still in play. "Whose move is it?"

"His. I guess I keep hoping that one day I'll look over and find that he's played. It's the same with the puzzle there. I don't guess I'll ever finish it. We kept that one on the board so I could move it back and forth to his bed when he got too sick to get up." She had a faraway look in her eyes. "He loved puzzles. He taught me to love them, too."

"I guess that's why you're a detective. Crimes are your puzzles."

She met his eyes, but her stare was empty. "Maybe. But mostly because when he'd tell me about his cases, it was like we were sharing secrets. He'd tell me the evidence and let me figure out who did it. I got really good at it and even found a few missing pieces. That's when I learned about cold cases. Agent Reed would send old files down, and Robert and I would pore over them for hours at a time. I watched a lot of Court TV, and before long, there was nothing else in the world I wanted to be. By the time I graduated high school, I'd helped him solve five murders and one cold case. I even helped find a missing girl once."

"Yeah? Was she alive?"

"No, she was dead. She'd been to a slumber party and wasn't there when the other girls woke up. The older brother had lured her up to his attic room, given her some alcohol to loosen her up, and then claimed that she walked out of the house to get some air. But three weeks into her being missing, I told Reed that I would check the brother's room again. And when they did, the odor was so strong that Reed called in backup immediately. She had been wrapped in heavy plastic and stuffed in an old suitcase that he'd piled a bunch of old newspapers on in the corner."

"She was there with him the whole time?"

Lizzy nodded. "Yes, it taught me a lesson in how some things can be right under our noses. As you can imagine, I won Agent Reed's heart. He got the credit, of course, with Robert being retired and in no way supposed to be sharing cases with a young girl he'd taken in."

"That's why you're so close to Sam Reed? You gave him the leg up first?"

She smiled and gave a nod. "I did. He was intrigued by me and my abilities, and honestly, being here with Robert and working on those cases, it was the first time anyone gave a damn about my opinions."

"What an amazing story. Much better than why I wanted to become a cop."

"Let's unpack the car, put away those groceries we picked up, and see if we can't make dinner out of them. I bought bread and cheese, and if I'm not mistaken, there is a can of tomato soup I left in the cabinet three months ago on my last trip if you're interested?"

"Sounds good. And then will you tell me more about Robert?"

"Only if you do me the honor of helping me finish that puzzle." She gestured to the coffee table and then turned and headed for the door.

Darek followed and helped her unpack the car. The two spent the next half hour getting settled and grilling cheese sandwiches and heating soup.

When they were done, they carried their dishes to the couch where Lizzy dunked her grilled cheese in the soup and took a bite. "I've wanted to finish this puzzle for a while now, and I never like to finish them alone."

"Your husband didn't like puzzles?" He'd never asked much about her marriage.

"No, he didn't like much of anything really. We weren't that compatible." She leaned over and picked up a piece and studied it. The puzzle was more than half-done, but one large corner remained.

"All of these pieces look the same to me," Darek said.

"You have to look for the subtle differences. See, this one has some of the water on it?"

He glanced around the room. "Where's the lid to the box? I need a guide."

"You can't look at the big picture, detective. That would be cheating." She gave him a sly grin. "Besides, Robert always threw away the box. He liked to glue the pieces together when they were finished and hang them in the study."

"You have a study?"

"Well, everyone else calls it a home office, but Robert called it his study." She rolled her eyes to heaven and back as if to see him. She put the piece in place, and then before long, she had two more pieces added.

Darek couldn't find one piece, but he kept trying. "I say we turn this thing around." The puzzle was upside down. "Get a different perspective."

"Nope, against the rules." She shook her head and looked even more determined than before. "Looking at it from this direction keeps you from being distracted by what's too common."

He wondered if everything was a lesson. "Did he have you wash and wax his cars, too? Wax on, wax off?"

She covered her mouth and laughed with the last bite of her sandwich in her cheeks. "You're going to make me choke, and then I'll never solve this case."

"You mean the puzzle?" Darek asked.

"No, the case. The killings. What we didn't find shit on today. It's going to take divine intervention for me to get a lead. No wonder Gough never had a chance. I'm sure the local detectives were in way over their heads."

"Or, and this is just a thought so don't get angry with me, but maybe it's because Gough was guilty."

She pushed another piece into the puzzle. "No. It's just all too much of a coincidence. You have Tad and these brands and this fucking Camp Victory, where no telling what the previous owners were doing to small boys. If I could link the pedophile ring to that club, or at least find a reason that links Tad to it, I'd be happy."

"You mean you're still going to pursue it? Camp V, I mean?"

"If I can find the old staff, you bet your ass. I'll also make a drive down on the weekend if I have to. I want that list of names, and there has to be someone willing to talk, someone who remembers something from when Tad was there. One of the names on that list could have done that to him. That person could be our killer." She put another piece in the puzzle and then tilted her head.

Darek looked down and saw the picture finally coming together. His heart turned to stone as he looked at the depiction of an old mill-house, not unlike the one at Camp V, only the one on the puzzle appeared to still be in working condition.

10

BAY

Bay hoped that his plans were well underway with Finn, and while the man was busy getting the dirt he needed, he had to check on a call that had come in during his family dinner. Lila had been livid that he was leaving, but he told her he'd deal with her later and made her retreat to her bedroom until he returned home. Her pregnancy had her testing her boundaries, and while he hadn't been the one to start their little collared-fantasy game, he was going to give her everything she wanted from it.

As he pulled up to the gate outside the white brick house, his mind switched from the bitch at home to a more pressing matter. He called his hired man, Lou, so he'd open the gate, and a moment later, he pulled into the circle drive of the old home which had once been a mansion in the seventies.

He parked the car in the garage, and when he got out, Lou came out to join him. The man looked tired, but he was stuffing his face with a piece of bread, so Bay knew he was good. All it took to keep Lou happy was plenty of pasta, a fully-stocked kitchen, and enough beer to drown an elephant.

"How's she doing, Lou?"

The man shrugged. "She's been screaming her fucking head off for hours. I can't tell you how bad I'd like to shove something in that mouth of hers."

"You go near her mouth with your cock or anything else, and I'll break your fucking neck."

"Don't worry. I like my paycheck too much. But can't we gag her or something?"

"We'll see. I hoped she would've calmed down by now." Bay walked through the kitchen from the garage and then past the great room down the hall to a door that led to the basement.

Bay stopped in his tracks. "Why is it fucking dark down here?"

"I shut out the lights and told her she couldn't have them back on until she shut the fuck up." Lou shoved the last bite of bread in his mouth.

"And I don't hear screaming, so why haven't you remedied this?" Bay was losing his patience with Lou, but he couldn't find anyone else willing to do the job for the chump change he was paying.

"Sorry, Boss. I got busy cooking dinner."

"Have you fed her, or just that fat fucking face of yours?" He met the man's eyes with his evil stare. "Go and get her a goddamned plate." Lou walked away, and Bay hit the light switch on his way down.

He turned the corner at the bottom of the stairs and found Hannah running full speed at him. He backed up just in time, and her leg chain tripped her as she ran out of slack.

"Fuck!" She held her ankle, and he walked over and knelt down beside her. Her hair was stringy, and she hadn't made use of the shower. He considered telling her that the cuff around her ankle wouldn't rust, but he had a feeling she wanted to be filthy, that it made her feel safe.

"Play nice, Hannah. I'm trying to help you, believe it or not. I could have already put you out of your misery and sent you home to Tad and Jesus, but I'm hoping you'll calm down and see things my way."

"Let me go!" She bared her teeth, and her eyes were so red, she looked like a demon.

"I've tried to make you comfortable here," Bay said. "You have a shower, a toilet, a bed; more than most prisoners." He wanted to add that Logan didn't even have his own shower, but he wanted her to ask about him herself. "Lou is going to bring you some food. I thought I'd come down and see how my favorite captive is doing. Did you eat your breakfast today?"

She pointed to the wall, and he growled when he saw the oatmeal stuck to the sheetrock. "Fuck your breakfast, asshole. Let me out of here."

"That's not nice, Hannah." He shook his head and gave a little *tsk* with his tongue.

"Fine." She met his eyes. "Fuck your breakfast, *Bay*."

"That's more like it." He stood up and then paced the room.

"Let me go or kill me already. Do you really think I'm afraid to die? Do you think you're doing anything but pissing me off?"

"Easy now. I came to try and talk sense to you. I know you heard all about Camp V, but that was so long ago, Hannah. Life's different, and it would benefit you well to just listen to reason. I know you liked me once, and I'm still that same man."

"It was a long time ago, Bay. You make me sick. I saw what you did to my brother. You dragged him down, and I'm pretty sure you're the one who pushed him out of that window."

"Don't be silly. I simply suggested it would be best for everyone, and then I left him alone to make his own decisions."

Hannah broke down in tears, her face puffy and swollen from all the crying she'd done since he'd taken her that night. She'd been easy to take, and after bugging Logan's studio, it was easy to see her comings and goings.

"Stop it, love. I hate to see a woman in tears unless my dick is buried in her throat."

"You like this, don't you? I heard all about how you get off to torturing people."

"I was hoping you'd play my way, Hannah. I need someone like you on my side. Someone who is willing to get things done, no matter what it takes. I can pay you handsomely for that kind of boldness.

You'll never want for anything again. Besides, I told your brother that I'd take good care of you. I didn't even tell him about how easy you spread. Just like butter." He licked his lips and grinned.

She shuddered. "It was one time, and that was before I knew what a monster asshole you are." She got to her knees and crawled back to her corner.

Bay shook his finger at her. "It wasn't just one time. It was three times. That morning head was the best. You sucked my dick better than anyone."

The growl that left her throat made him smile. "Yet you didn't like it enough to call me back. Save your breath. I'll never be with you. You want me, you'll have to kill me first. You'd probably like that, wouldn't you?"

He didn't appreciate the vulgar insinuation. Even he had his standards. "If I wanted to violate you, Hannah, I could have already. And if I were a monster, I'd have already let Lou and the others I have watching this house have you any way they pleased. Instead, I keep you safe."

"You should be so fucking proud of yourself. You've got good deeds and kidnapping confused again."

"You seem hellbent. I guess I'll just leave you alone until I can figure out what to do with you." He walked to the stairs and stopped. "Until then, you're safe."

"I have work. People will be looking for me! The police will come. They'll find me."

"They aren't in too big a hurry. You see, they think you're dead. They found your car out by the tracks with blood in it. Add that to the fact that your brother turned up dead, and your uncle, and you'll be pushed to the back of the line. A dead body doesn't get resources. They'll assume someone will find you once you start to decompose, but they've got too many other criminals in this city to keep them busy. Why do you think they were so quick to assume Tad killed your uncle and that Logan killed his other girlfriend? Speaking of Logan, aren't you even concerned about him? Don't you even want to know what happened? He asked me about you, you know?"

"Fuck you. You're both killers."

"He's being transferred to the penitentiary," Bay said. "He's scared you're dead, but I told him you probably ran off to be away from him. Staged your own death, so to speak." He liked toying with her about Logan, mostly because he was a little bitter that she gave herself to him.

"I don't care about him anymore. I had just let myself love him when he told me, so it didn't take much to come to my senses."

"And yet, he pines for you from his prison cell." He chuckled. "How pathetic. I would be willing to overlook that moment of weakness, especially since I found out that you used sex to make him spill a decade old secret. I have to say, that was pretty fucking impressive, and a total turn on. Further proof we'd be a good team."

"I'm not like you," she snapped. "I'm not ever going to hurt people like you do. I'm a nurse. It's not in my nature."

With that confession, he wondered why he'd even bothered. Surely, she was more of a nurturer than a deviant like he was, but he'd really hoped that he would be able to keep her around as long as possible. "I do wish this had turned out better. Enjoy your dinner." He turned around and took a few steps.

"Wait, no wait!" She got to her feet as Bay turned, and she limped across the room, closing the distance between them. "Please, Bay. Please. I'll do anything, just let me go. I'll play nice; I'll give you what you want." She lifted her shirt and Bay smiled as she cupped her heavy breasts. "We can fuck, Bay. I'll fuck you right now."

He shook his head. She didn't get it at all, and her offer was more insulting than a fucking turn on. "What I want is your sworn fealty."

He turned and left her alone to think it over, not as convinced that he would win her over as he'd been when he first entered the room.

On his way out, he passed Lou who was carrying a big tray of food. "How's this, boss?" The pasta dish smelled amazing, and there was even a slice of French bread that the man hadn't scarfed down for himself.

Bay took the fork from the plate and left the spoon. "That's better, and no more lights out. Let her scream at the top of her lungs if she wants to. No one will hear her." He reached into the bowl and grabbed a saucy noodle and gave it a taste. "Not bad, Lou."

On his way out, he got a call from Finn. "Tell me you're not backing out? You're not going to choke, are you?" Bay had jokes for days, but they went right over Finn's head. He'd always been a bit dim, but he was loyal, and that was all that mattered to Bay.

"I did it," Finn said, still breathless from his tryst.

"Very good. I'll meet you at the penthouse in half an hour." He shut off the phone and wondered what kind of footage Finn got and if it would be enough to ruin a campaign and worth enough to pay for a movie. He might just have to rethink the latter and shortchange him. The deed was done, and he highly doubted that Finn would put up a fight. The movie was going to be shit anyway, and he knew anything he put into it, he'd never get back. He really wished he'd never made the deal, but if he had Seth on film getting blown in a deviant sex act, it might be worth it.

11

FINN

Finn couldn't believe what he'd done for Bay, and while he waited for Bay's car to pull up at the penthouse, which he'd managed to get to first, he couldn't tune out the thoughts in his head.

He didn't mind what he'd done, but once he'd done it, he realized that not only was Seth on the film but so was he. Whatever ammo he was giving Bay could come back to haunt him, too.

He's never going to pay me. He's going to use the fucking tape against me, too. Stupid, stupid, stupid. Finn had let his desires get in the way of his common sense, and he let his trust in Bay weaken him. Just like before.

Finn had always been the more sensitive type, and Bay loved to aggravate him because of it, but when they were alone, Bay would always tell Finn that he was just fooling and that Finn shouldn't be so tenderhearted when it came to him. The night of the ritual, when Finn had choked, Bay had pulled him aside.

Bay had left Seth in charge, and the two had walked out and around to the other side of the millhouse to stand in the moonlight. Finn had needed air, but Bay had been afraid he was going to bail.

Bay placed his hand on the boy's back. "You can't back out now, Finn. I thought you liked me."

"I do. I'm your friend, Bay, but I can't do it. She won't stop scream-ing." He had covered his ears before walking out, and he knew the other boys were having just as much trouble with the sounds. Several wanted it to end as much as him.

"You took a vow, and this is going to bond us even tighter. I hoped it meant something to you more than the rest."

Finn turned his eyes up, and his breath hitched as he noticed how strikingly beautiful the creature before him was. Bay's hair shone in the moonlight, and he radiated like a star. "Why me?"

Bay took his hand. "I thought my feelings were obvious, Finn. Yours are." His voice was a whisper, and he looked back to the mill-house where the moans of the girl were still audible through the old stone walls.

"I don't know what you mean."

"I guess I was wrong, then. I guess I just hoped that what I wanted was true about you." Bay pulled his hand away, and Finn felt an emptiness inside.

"I *do* feel the same. I do. I'm just scared. I'm scared the others will laugh."

"They will, Finn, but not me. I'll never laugh. This can be our secret, this longing we feel. It can be our special thing." Bay's breath was warm as he whispered close to Finn, and Finn knew that he would never want another human being's approval like he wanted Bay's.

"Do you really mean it?" Finn asked. "You feel the same?" He had never thought he'd find anyone who wanted to be with him the same way, who wasn't afraid of getting caught and wouldn't see it as some-thing dirty. He and Seth had only explored together a little bit, and only once had it gotten to the point where Finn had been brave enough to blow him. Finn hoped that he and Bay could have so much more.

But Bay had been nothing more than a tease ever since.

Bay arrived at the penthouse, pulling up in his fancy fucking car in one of his fancy fucking suits, which looked like it had been specially fitted to make Finn want him even more.

Finn got out of the car and approached Bay's car as he opened the door.

"Come on," Bay said. "Let's get inside. Neither of us should be standing around in dark places at night."

Bay had a point, and without further ado, they went inside the building and got into the elevator.

"Do you have it?" Bay asked, holding out his hand.

Finn hesitated. "I just thought that I'd like to edit this footage. My identity is on it as well, and no offense, but I'd like to get it off of there before anyone sees it."

"Still ashamed of who you are, I see."

"Fuck you. I'm as straight as you are. I just happen to have an unhealthy affection for you."

"Please, what you have is a fetish for dick. I won't judge, mind you, but let's stop pretending you're not as queer as a three-dollar-bill." The elevator came to a stop, and when the door opened on their floor, Finn stood against the back wall as Bay stepped out to his entrance. "What the fuck are you waiting for? Let's go."

"No, you've told me all I needed to hear," Finn said. "I'm not giving you this footage to use against me. Call me any slur you want, but I'm not stupid. If you play nice, I'll give you an edited copy."

Bay squared his shoulders and then held the door. "Get out of the fucking elevator before I drag you by your dick and beat the shit out of you."

"Can't you even ask nicely?"

Bay's nostrils flared. "Don't fuck with me tonight, Finn. You made a deal. You'd get me this footage, and then I'd finance your fucking film."

"You're a fucking tease. I think you're all talk, and you're obviously afraid to have me because you know you're going to like it."

Bay stormed into the elevator and grabbed his throat. "Do you think I need you for sex? I could take you any fucking time I want since we were fucking fourteen years old, but have I? Fuck no, and you know why?"

"Because you're a fucking liar." Finn thought back to all the times when he'd flirted and lured. He'd always had some kind of excuse not to go through with it, and Finn had tried to be understanding. He'd pined away for him like a fool, loving him even though he was never going to get anything in return.

Bay met his eyes. "No, it's because you don't trust me." He let go of Finn's throat and stepped back out. He went to his penthouse and opened the door.

Finn hurried out of the elevator and pushed his way inside. "I want to trust you. So, let me edit the footage."

"Fine, but if you trusted me, you wouldn't feel the need."

"Here." Finn handed him his phone and took a deep breath as Bay turned on the replay.

"You're really committed to your mission. Impressive."

Finn pulled the device from him, but Bay had already removed the tiny camera from the side. "Send me the file." Bay gave him his warmest smile.

Finn growled under his breath but gave in. "Fine!"

While Finn prepared to send the file, Bay took out his phone. "Check this out."

"Holy shit, is that Ethan Cline?" Finn would have recognized the Zodiac's Virgo anywhere. He still had the same shit-eating smile and was apparently, according to the headline above his picture, having the worst luck with the ladies. The article said that he was having trouble with his model girlfriend.

Bay belly laughed, which was rare. "He's working the more popular girlfriend angle, which apparently backfired."

"I had heard he was doing well in Nashville, but I didn't know *that* well." Finn wasn't much on his old friend's music, but he couldn't deny his talent. It was good to see someone else succeeding, even though it made him all the more anxious for his movie. He knew he needed to be focused on his art, but it was too hard while he was in New York and so close to Bay Collins.

Bay was busy scrolling through the article. "Yeah, he kind of took the whole *Carpe Fortuna* motto and ran with it." Bay laughed and then walked over and sat on the couch. "Have a seat."

"Thanks." Finn wasn't about to forget the things Bay had said, and he knew he should be leery of letting him get too close, but he just couldn't help himself. He looked at the man and saw the only person he'd longed for in his life, not only to be with but to be *like*. People looked up to Bay. They listened to him, respected him, adored him, and some even worshiped him. Finn's heart ached every time he looked at him. "Why do you and Seth hate each other?"

"Hate isn't accurate," Bay said. "I don't really have feelings for him one way or the other. He dislikes me because he always thought that he should lead the Zodiacs. Even though it was my idea. He just always felt like he could run it better. The truth is, he wouldn't last a fucking day with some of you. He has no business leading anyone or anything, especially in politics." Bay chuckled softly as he stared at the phone.

Finn hit send on his own phone, and it only took seconds for the file to arrive in Bay's phone. "Thanks. I won't let anyone see it. I promise. It's just leverage for Seth when I need it."

Finn tried to act like it didn't bother him. "Okay." He still wasn't sure he could trust Bay, but he couldn't fight him, either.

It grew quiet, and then Bay gave him a nudge. "I'm sorry I grabbed your throat. I'm pretty sure it's sore enough already." He smirked, the slow smile spreading his lips.

Finn let loose a breath and rolled his eyes. The jokes were getting to be too much. "Seriously?"

Bay's charming smile widened. "Come on, man. You're the only one I can joke with. Do you think I sit down and talk to the others about anything? No, I don't. Not ever, and do you know why?"

"Why?" He hoped that Bay would move closer and tell him how special he was, but that wasn't going to happen, not tonight. He could tell that Bay was already too distant.

"Because the others are assholes. You're a good guy. You come from a good family. You're talented. You're way more of a man than most of them." He could listen to Bay talk about him forever, but he knew that didn't mean he wanted him for anything more.

"So, are you going to fund my movie?" Finn asked. At this point, it was all he cared about anyway. He didn't have room to feel too much about Bay.

"I suppose I should keep my word. But only on one condition."

There were always conditions with Bay Collins. No one simply got anything for free. That just didn't happen. "What condition?"

"You leave my name off the credits." Bay could be terribly insulting, but Finn didn't care. He wasn't going to let the man ruin his excitement.

"It's a deal. Probably best that you're not associated with me anyway, considering the whole Zodiac thing. Did you get any more news?"

"About what?" Bay laid his head back and closed his eyes as if he'd had a long day.

"The killings. Have you heard anything more?"

"No, but it's okay. I told you, if anyone is the target, it's Logan. I'm sure the killer is just trying to find a way to get to him in prison. Probably waiting for him to get nice and cozy." Something about Bay's tone, the nonchalant way he spoke, gave Finn a sick feeling.

"You're not going to let anything happen to him, are you? I mean, you're his lawyer. You can do something, right? To assure his safety?"

Bay turned his head and met Finn's stare with a twisted smile. "Of course. Just like I look out for you all."

12

DAREK

Darek and Lizzy finished the puzzle and then put on some old movies that she and Robert used to love. Darek enjoyed the trip down memory lane with her and hoped that he would learn more about the amazing woman he was falling head over heels for.

He was finally willing to admit it to himself, and he knew that it was only a matter of time before passion beat out his common sense.

He busied himself cleaning the kitchen while Lizzy was at the other end of the house.

"I put clean sheets on the guest bed," she said when she returned to the kitchen. "I'm going to take my old room."

He noticed that she didn't want to stay in the master suite, where no doubt Robert had taken his last breaths. "Thank you. That's perfect."

She nodded. "I know it's kind of silly since we've shared a bed, but I know that went against your better judgment."

"Yeah, but I don't regret it. Do you?"

"No, but you're right," Lizzy said. "If you're going to move up and start working at the Bureau, it's best we're not sleeping together."

He agreed, but he wished to hell he'd kept his big mouth shut.

But on the other hand, he was glad she was okay with it. "It's bad timing."

"Yes, totally." She walked over and took the sponge from his hand. "You don't have to clean up."

"I don't mind." He took the sponge back. "It's the least I can do. Besides, you made a mess with the soup. It looks like someone bled all over the stove."

She laughed and then leaned in and gave him a quick peck. "I'll be right out."

He finished up in the kitchen, and while he wiped his hands, his neck itched. He tugged at his collar. The damned thing must have had something in it. He'd itched all damned day. He tried to ignore it and went to the study as the water came on in the shower down the hall.

Robert had a nice study with a big mahogany desk and lots of plaques from achievements throughout his life and time with the Bureau. Across the room, there was a pair of chairs, and between them was a small table with a stone top that was covered with glass. Inside were several hunting knives and a few merit badges with a lucky rabbit's foot. There was a file cabinet behind the desk, and he couldn't help but wonder if it was the old case files a much younger Lizzy had worked on.

He hated to snoop, but he just might find out more about Lizzy and her father. He had a feeling the asshole abused her, and if not sexually, then mentally and verbally. He'd noticed that throughout the night, no matter how many times he tried to ask about her parents, she'd steer the conversation back to Robert. Were her memories of home so painful that she couldn't even speak of them?

The cabinet, along with most of the desk drawers, were locked, but he noticed a basket with a stack of old newspapers and decided to give them a look. Midway through the stack, he came to an article about Emily Johnson's murder and Gough's prison sentence. The papers were in fairly decent shape, and he wondered if Lizzy had forgotten she had them.

"Finding anything interesting?"

Darek looked up, and Lizzy was standing in the doorway wearing an FBI tee and a pair of yoga pants. Her hair was still damp and pulled away from her face.

"Sorry, I just thought I'd look around. I hope it wasn't a big deal."

"Not at all. Those old papers have been there forever."

"And here's one you might want to see." He held up the old article, not thinking it could contain anything she hadn't seen before.

She walked over, and her face fell as she looked at the write-up. "I'll have to take this and add it to my evidence." She tucked the paper up under her arm and then took Darek's hand. "I'm going to bed. Thank you for an amazing day." She kissed his hand, and he reached up and stroked her cheek.

"Sorry, it didn't all go as planned. I know you were hoping to get a lot more from this trip."

"Yeah, well, I guess it could have been worse. At least I got to see the lay of the land, and now, I'm even more convinced that somehow she ended up running into one of those boys. Maybe Tad Halston. Maybe someone else. He could have met her there when she got off work the night before. I don't know. They are just so much closer than I even thought they'd be, so close that the Gas and Guzzle manager had to put up a fence to keep them from coming to his store."

Darek shrugged. "You know kids. They like to go to those places and pick up a pop. That doesn't make them killers."

"It doesn't mean they're not, either." She held up a finger to prove her point. "I'm going to bed."

"Wait for me." He got up from the desk and followed behind her. "You're just next door, right? I mean, in case I wake up scared in an unfamiliar place?" He tried to be flirty, but she let go of his hand and walked to her door.

"I'll be right in here." She opened the door, and once she shut the door, he went into his room and did the same. He was just settling in bed when he heard a knock.

"Darek?" Lizzy opened the door, and he rolled over to see her, thankful that he'd slept in a white T-shirt and shorts and not bare-chested for her to see his Zodiac symbol.

"Hey, is something wrong?" he asked. The room was dark, but she didn't bother turning on the lights.

"I guess being here is harder than I thought. I guess it got too quiet, and I started thinking too much."

"I know it can't be easy," he said.

"He died across the hall. I was with him, holding his hand to comfort him. He was alert right up to the end." She said the words in a monotone voice, and he held out the covers for her to join him.

"Come lay with me. We'll practice our spooning."

She crossed the room and sat on the edge of the bed. "You must think I'm weak."

"No way. I think it takes an incredibly strong woman to not only take care of someone who is dying, but to hold their hand when they go. You shouldn't feel weak."

"Thank you. I just feel so silly for coming in here. I don't want you to think I'm up to something."

"I hope you are. It's when you're not up to something that I'll start to worry." He rolled over and pulled the covers back. "Come on, Lizzy. Snuggle with me. I'll be a perfect gentleman if you want."

She stretched out beside him, putting her cold feet against his. "And what if I don't want you to be a perfect gentleman?" Her hand snaked around his waist, her nails grazing his back through his shirt.

"I'm afraid I'd have to oblige. I'm not really good at self-control." Especially when it came to her. The woman drove him mad.

"That's what I'm counting on." She lifted her leg across his hip, and he rubbed her thigh and ass, giving it a squeeze as she moved closer and kissed him.

He deepened the kiss, and she closed the space between them, their bodies pressing close to one another, gyrating and working up nice, warm friction.

He could tell that the heat was getting to be too much and pulled the covers away from himself. Lizzy kicked them the rest of the way off, and he took the chance to move on top of her.

He made love to her lips and then trailed down to her breasts and lower. When he nestled between her legs, she placed her hand on his head and then ran her fingers through his hair.

"Darek?"

"Yeah? Fuck, Lizzy. I'm sorry. Is this okay?" He hadn't really expected things to go this far, but there they were, working up enough heat that he was about to lose his clothes and peel hers from her, too.

"Yes, it's more than okay."

He pressed his hard cock against her center, and she moaned. "Are you sure?" he asked. He needed her to know what she was up against, and that even if it wasn't the right time, and even if it was a huge mistake for the two of them to hook up, he wasn't going to stop. The room was dark enough, and he'd keep his shirt close just in case, but he needed to feel her flesh against his own. He'd waited too long for something this real, and she'd been tempting him all fucking day.

"Yes, please, Darek. We don't have to tell a soul. What Sam Reed doesn't know won't stop you from that promotion."

"I'd tell the world if I could, but it wouldn't do either of us any good. That's why I need you to be sure you want this. I'm not going to be able to stop sneaking around with you, Lizzy. But that's what it's going to be. You know it, and I know it."

"I know, and I don't care. I'd rather sneak than not have you at all."

He pulled off her shirt, and her hands went under him as he cupped her breasts and ground against her.

When he couldn't stand it anymore, he stripped off her yoga pants and went down on her. He pressed his nose against her, his tongue darting out to taste her honey as his fingers dipped into her slick channel.

She hissed through her teeth and moaned, and he continued to work her through her first release, which soaked his palm. She was so beautiful, inside and out, that he ached for more.

He rose up, resting on his elbows, grinding his hips into her as she shrugged his shorts down around his ass. His cock sprang free and his heated flesh rested on her bare hip. He was inches away from being buried inside her, and once he took the plunge, there was no going back.

He didn't hesitate. He moved to her center and rested his head just inside her, pushing it against her slit where the warmth and wetness were an invitation. He'd never liked to mix business with pleasure, but Lizzy was different. He was going to make her pleasure his business, at least for the next few hours.

He nudged his way inside her slick heat. "Fuck, you feel amazing, Lizzy."

She closed her legs around his ass and pulled him toward her to encourage him deeper. "It certainly does. Surely makes up for a shitty day of investigating." She cried out as he sank deeper, the pleasure-filled moan rolling from her throat only making him want to hear it again.

Everything about her was perfect, every whimper, every purr, right down to the way her smooth thighs felt around his waist. He settled deep inside her, sinking his cock balls-deep, and then grinding against her clit until she shuddered, settling around his girth. He gave her a minute to adjust and then pulled his hips back, thrusting slowly, building up his rhythm with every thrust.

Her nails went up his back, and before he knew it, his shirt came up, the cold air hitting his back as she pulled it over his head and tossed it to the floor. In the darkness, he didn't even care. He needed to be real with her. To forget the awful past and all the lies. He felt like he could finally be himself, not Darek the detective, not Darek with the dark past. He finally felt free. However fleeting the moment would be, however little it would reveal about himself to her, he would not relent until they were both sated. He owed her that much; he owed it to himself.

13

DAREK

Darek could barely sleep, and he itched so badly that he sneaked out of his bed and into the bathroom to shower just before the sun came up. Wiping the steam from the mirror, he caught his reflection and panicked. A red rash has spread across his neck, and the first thing that came to mind was his fall out by the old millhouse.

"Son of a bitch."

He dried off and dressed, trying his hardest not to wake Lizzy in the process. He hoped that she wasn't allergic to whatever he'd gotten into, and he went back to the bathroom to check his crotch to make sure he hadn't spread it to any other parts of his body. Thankfully, everything was good, and the only heat he'd had on his cock in the past day was Lizzy.

He looked up some rashes on his phone and tried to see if it was a match to his, but that just got him a bunch of horrible images he couldn't un-see. "Dammit," he cursed as he took one more look in the mirror.

"Are you okay in there?"

When he opened the door, he found Lizzy wrapped up in a sheet and looking like a goddess.

"Yeah, sorry," he said. "It seems I got into something yesterday. Please tell me you're not allergic to poison ivy or oak. I have a feeling that's what this is."

The owners of Camp Victory had worked hard to keep it out of their campsite back in the day, or at least, so he'd heard, but no one bothered to think about the millhouse area located behind the camp.

"I don't think so," Lizzy said. "At least, I've never had any problems. Robert and I used to work in the yard a lot and even did some exploring through the woods and down the creek, but then again, I never went rolling around on the ground, either." She looked at his neck and cringed. "That's a nasty rash. Did it spread?"

"No, but you may want to check yourself. I didn't feel it this intensely yesterday."

"Maybe all that exertion from last night made it kick in." She opened her sheet and dropped it to the floor. "Check me out and see if you see anything." She held out her arms and turned in a circle as if modesty wasn't in her vocabulary.

"Perfection. Nothing out of place. I didn't even leave a mark on you." He gave her a wink.

She took his hand and put it on her waist. "I wouldn't say that. I *am* walking a little funny this morning." She brought her lips to his for a quick kiss and then turned away.

"I'd have you on your back again already if I wasn't afraid of giving you the itch. The ride home is going to suck with all this scratching."

"Why don't you soak in the tub and let me run into town and get you some lotion? I'll grab some stuff from the store, drop some money by the caretaker's house, and then I'll come back and make you a nice lunch before we get on the road."

"I like the sound of that, but are you sure you don't need me to ride along?"

"I grew up here. I'll be fine." She brushed his hair from his forehead. "Don't scratch while I'm gone. You'll make it worse."

He didn't mind her going out without him and thought it might give him a little time to make a few calls and check the burner phone in her absence. "I'll behave."

Before she left the bathroom, she bent over the tub, giving him a nice long look at her ass. "There. It's just the right temperature." She gave him a kiss, then bent over to pick up her sheet. As she disappeared into the bedroom down the hall, he shut the door and locked it before getting undressed.

He sat on the side of the tub and dunked his feet in the water as he went through his phone. He found a number there he hadn't expected to use again. The phone rang and Marie, the only dermatologist he knew, answered.

"Detective Blake?"

He thought the woman might not have his name saved, but the fact that she did made him a little suspicious that she still had a crush on him. He didn't want to send any unintended signals, and this woman was a bit of a wildcard. "Yeah, it's me. I hate to call you up out of the blue on a Sunday morning with business, but I've gotten into something, and I need to see you tomorrow if at all possible."

"Anything for you, Detective. Just show up around one, and I'll fit you in. But, just to satisfy my curiosity, what is the problem?"

"I think it's poison ivy, but I can't be sure. I fell into some weeds yesterday, and I have an ugly, itchy rash on my shoulder."

"Don't scratch it," she said sternly. "Keep it clean and put some calamine lotion on it. I'll take a look and make sure it's not something else."

"Thanks, Marie. I can't focus on work if I'm busy scratching." He wanted to keep it as much about business as possible.

"Well, I'll cure your itches." She giggled. "See you then."

He heard Lizzy's car leaving and got up from the tub. He wasn't going to spend the entire fucking time she was gone soaking, and it wasn't like he'd be neck deep in the fucking tub anyway, but he thought it best to humor her and let her go on without him.

He went back to his bedroom where he'd stashed his bag, and he found the other phone, which he'd silenced before stuffing into a pocket on his bag. He looked for a new message, but there wasn't anything new. He moved to stow it away in the bag when it went off in his hand, giving him a start.

"Fuck!" He held his hammering heart. "Motherfucker."

He saw a message from the killer, and when he opened the message fully, it read: *Hope you enjoyed your little vacation. Time to get back to work.* The message ended with two little fish emojis.

"Pisces," he said as a chill ran down his back.

The killer was going to give him something to come home to. He called Bay, hoping he could warn Finn or at least give Darek the guy's number. He needed to be warned, and maybe Darek could talk him into leaving New York. He could always go back to California and be away from all of the chaos. So far, the killer had only been working in New York, so Finn could go home and have nothing to worry about.

Darek hit the button to call Bay Collins and sat on the end of the bed where he could see when Lizzy returned.

"Don't tell me you have another question about Camp V," Bay said instead of saying hello. He gave a bored laugh, and Darek wondered if there was anything else he'd gone out of his way to cover up. Bay had certainly been a lot busier than Darek had expected over the years.

"No, I just wanted to know if Finn's in town."

"Yes, he's still hanging around, and so was Seth."

"Seth was in town? Why? He's Aries, isn't he?"

"Yeah, rather unfortunate for him. Horrible timing." Bay chuckled softly.

"Had you not warned him about the killings? Or is that what made him curious?" Knowing Seth's ego, he came to New York to dare the killer. If anyone was as egotistical as Bay, it was Seth.

"He was in town for a little action, but don't worry. He's already on his way back to Dallas. Took a flight out late last night. So, what do you need to call Finn about?"

"I just got a warning that he's on the killer's radar."

"Oh? Is he? And what about Logan? I guess the killer is going to let him off the hook?"

"Perhaps the killer thinks that taking his freedom is enough of a payback? I don't know. All I know is, you can either warn Finn, or I will."

"I'll take care of it, but hey, what kind of warning did you get?" Bay's voice was steeped with suspicion.

"Don't worry about it. I have my ways, and that's all you need to know."

"You know, I don't like this new attitude of yours, Darek. You, the killer, and even the guys, you're all underestimating me, keeping me out of the loop. It's all very hurtful and rather annoying."

"Sorry if I hurt your feelings," Darek said, knowing that Bay wouldn't miss the sarcasm in his tone. The man barely *had* feelings, and if he felt anything, it was a betrayal. Either way, Darek couldn't care any less. "Could you please just get the message to Finn? When is he leaving town?"

"He's here until midweek. I have him doing a little job for me, and after that, I'm going to turn him loose."

Darek couldn't imagine what kind of deal he'd made with the man. Whatever it was, Darek hoped Bay would help protect his interests by keeping Finn safe.

"Tell him I said hello and to be in touch if he hears from the killer at all." Darek hung up the phone without any farewell and then got up and changed his clothes so Lizzy would feel like he'd done something. He walked around the room, gathering his few belongings and put them in his bag so he'd be ready to leave Maryland for home.

After he finished, he went to Lizzy's room to look around. It was hard to believe she'd grown up there by the looks of the room. It wasn't decorated like he'd expected a young girl's room to be, with posters of boy bands or bulletin boards covered with photos of her and her besties. There were no stuffed animals or vanity tables, and the only thing remotely feminine was her bedding, which was a pretty purple floral set that matched her curtains. There was an old computer that looked like it had seen better days and a row of books that had a good layer of dust on them. He knew better than to disturb them but couldn't help notice the one on top was about famous true crimes. She'd been obsessed, even way back then.

The sound of her car returning brought his head around to the window, and he hurried out of the room, pulling the door closed as he'd found it.

He went out to offer a hand, but all she had was a takeout bag and a small paper bag from the pharmacy.

She shook the bag at him. "I got you a present for your itch." She met his mouth with a quick kiss. He was going to savor every one of them, knowing as soon as they got back to the office, those sweet kisses would be fewer and further between.

"Thanks, I called my dermatologist to make an appointment for tomorrow. I'm not taking any chances."

"I don't blame you. What did he say?"

"*She* is going to fit me in tomorrow," he said.

"Oh? Is *she* an old friend of yours?" She placed the bags of food on the counter.

"Yeah, I went to school with her, actually." He looked for an ounce of jealousy in her eyes but came up empty, which was a relief. He didn't want any problems with jealous women in his life. One fucking headcase in his life was enough, and that part had been filled by his ex-wife.

"That's good," Lizzy said. "Hopefully, she can tell you for sure what it is, but in the meantime, let's gets you doctored up. You want to take off your shirt?"

"No need. It's not anywhere else. Just my neck." Darek pulled his shirt collar out of the way.

Lizzy took his hand and brought him back down the hall to the bathroom where she got a cotton ball and applied the cream. "There. That should start to feel better."

"It does already. Thanks." He gave her another kiss, and she pulled away and dropped the cotton ball in the garbage.

"After we're done with lunch, we should really get back on the road. I have some paperwork to file, and I want to call Mr. Williford and see if he's remembered anything before I turn it in."

"Yeah, I guess this can't last forever, unless you want to run away with me and never look back?" He liked the sound of that.

"Maybe after we solve this case."

A sudden sick feeling hit his stomach, knowing if they solved it, there would be no future for them. When they go back to work, the dream would be over, and he'd be back to walking that tightrope, the one that was only going to lead to heartbreak. Hers and his.

14

FINN

Sunday wasn't any better than the rest of Finn's trip. He'd left Bay's penthouse in the early morning, but the man had never made a move to try and give him what he wanted. He should have known better than to ever think he would. But when his phone rang while he was leaving to meet with an artist for the movie, he was happy to see that is was Bay.

"What's up, Bay?"

"Just thought I'd call and warn you that our favorite detective just called and said that your head is on the chopping block."

"Very funny. If you're fucking with me, Bay, it's not cool." He didn't think it was funny at all, and to kid about it was to make a mockery of what had happened to their friends.

"I'm not kidding. I'm serious. I don't know where he's getting the information, he wouldn't tell me, but if he says so, you better believe it. If you don't, call him."

Finn's belief that Bay was fooling around faded, and panic slowly set in. "I've got places to be today, Bay. I can't be worried about this shit." He knew it was silly since his life was on the line, but so was his career. And if this bullshit ended up being just a shallow threat, he was going to be giving up a whole lot because of it. "Dammit. Should I go to this fucking meeting?"

"If it's about where I'm putting my goddamned money, you bet your sweet ass you should. Although, now I'm starting to reconsider the loan again. I don't want to hand you a wad of cash, and you get killed before I can recoup it."

"That's bullshit. I'm making the fucking movie, even if I have to go into hiding to do it. I'm going to get back home, and then I won't have to fucking worry about it."

"God, I knew you'd flip out and run home. Look, you have work to do. Not only do I want that fucking file of you and Seth edited, but I need you to get a good start on this project before I regret promising you the money."

"It's not like I don't want to, dammit, but for fuck's sake, Bay. Someone is out there gunning for me."

"I'll have my men tail you. They'll let me know if someone is after you or not, and maybe this way, we'll be able to find out who this motherfucker is."

"I'm a sitting duck here," Finn said.

"Fine, you can come stay here at the penthouse for a few days."

He couldn't believe the invitation and decided to take him up on it. "I'll pack my things, and when I'm done with my next meeting, I'll head over."

"Fine, I'll be here for a while. I have Mia coming over again."

Finn hated knowing that Bay was having his girlfriend around. Finn thought he and Bay would have more fun with Bay's wife than her younger sister. Still, he wouldn't pass up the chance to spend some more time around the man he was infatuated with, and to be fair, he would be a lot safer there than anywhere else in the city.

Finn packed up a few of his things to take along, and he called for help with the sculpture he'd bought from Logan and had it brought down to his car. Thankfully, it wasn't that big a deal, and the same men who helped him get it up to his room took it back and loaded it. He was going to have to take it into Bay's penthouse and hoped that he didn't mind.

Once he had his stuff situated, he checked out of the room and tipped the men handsomely for their help. He made it across town to his meeting and hoped this time he'd found a winner.

"Come in, come in," said Wes Finkle, the artist whom he hoped would take Logan's place. "Thanks for coming on a Sunday, my friend. You don't know what a lifesaver you are."

"Well, it helped me out, too," Finn said. "I'm afraid that I'll be leaving town soon, and I appreciate you arranging this so I could see your work in person."

"I'm always happy to show my work off." The man was flamboyant, and Finn didn't have to wonder if he were gay. The half-naked men depicted in the art around his studio told him that much, if his mannerisms and effeminate voice didn't. "I'm such a shameless bitch. You have to watch me."

Finn laughed along with the man, and when he walked into the back room where the man worked on his metal masterpieces, he knew this was his guy. The works weren't quite as intricate as the ones he'd ordered from Logan, but the man's style was close enough that he knew he could handle Finn's vision.

"Now I see why you want to show it off," Finn said. "You do amazing work."

"Thank you. My father wanted me to be an engineer, but I couldn't be the son he wanted. I had to spread my wings, and that's when I picked up a torch and turned our old lawn furniture into something amazing for my mother. Gave my father the red ass, but I didn't care." He spoke lively with his hands and patted Finn on the shoulder. "Sorry, I'm a bit hands-on. Hard not to be with a handsome fella like yourself. Are you married?"

"No, I'm seeing a woman in California where I'm from." Finn wanted to send a clear message to the man that he wasn't in the market, or even on the same playing field.

"Good for you. That's wonderful." The man seemed genuinely happy for him, and Finn felt like that was just what he needed, someone genuine to be involved with him. Someone passionate and confident. The man fit that description perfectly.

"Thanks," Finn said. "So, how would you like to take on a special project for my movie?"

"Really? You mean, you think it's what you're looking for?"

"I do. I really think your work is special, and I hope you're willing to put your flare on the specs when I send them. I'll have to call my investor, of course. He likes to see where his money is going, and then I'll call you and let you know the deadline if that's going to work for you."

Wes held his hands together as if it was all he could do to contain his excitement. "It more than works. I've been hoping for a special project."

"You've got one," Finn said. "I'll go make some calls, and then I'll come back here tonight with a check for the deposit if that's okay? I have another meeting with a special effects makeup artist, and of course, as you know, I'll be leaving town in a day or two, if not sooner. Life's crazy when you're making a movie."

"That's fine, and I understand. Thank you for the opportunity." Wes shook his hand and showed him out, and as Finn walked down, he thought it safer to be on the phone. He called Edie, who answered on the first ring.

"Please tell me you're coming home soon. I miss you terribly." Edie was using her baby voice again, talking to him like he was her pet golden retriever or worse, a two-month-old baby.

He suppressed his irritation. "I miss you, too. I just wanted to share the good news with you." She'd been working so hard for him, he knew she'd appreciate something happy for a change.

"Good news? Oh, what is it?" He could imagine her bouncing up and down in her seat as she did anytime he gave her good news, and he hoped she was, because she was due some happiness, too.

"I found an artist," he said. "He's just as good as the last one, and although his style is unique, it's similar to the one who fell through, so I think we're good to go. I've got to go talk to the investor, and then I will bring him his deposit and the specs tonight. I can't wait."

"Oh, honey, that's spectacular. I can't believe your luck has turned." She was always going on and on about his luck, but he had always made his own instead of depending on charms or prayers.

"If it's luck, then I'll take it. I like to think of it as hard work, and when that pays off, it's much more gratifying." He wasn't about to give luck all the credit.

"Did you find a makeup artist yet?"

"I have a person I'm meeting within an hour, but I'm going to have to find the designer closer to home, I think." He hadn't ever intended to fill all the positions he'd needed in a single trip, and now with these things situated, he at least felt confident enough to take Bay's money.

"I can't wait until you are home, baby. I have a surprise for you. You're going to love it." She had stopped using her baby voice and started using her more serious, sultry voice.

"Is that so?" he asked, thinking of how it would compare to all of the crazy kinks he'd been tied up with on the trip. He hadn't intended on hooking up with so many, but he and Raven had been having a wonderful time at the club.

"Yes, that's so." She said with an alluring tone. He had no idea what it could be and didn't care to know or to press.

"I love surprises, Edie. Miss you, darling." He got into his car and shut the door and locked it. "I should get to my next meeting. I'll call when I'm done."

"Oh, okay." She sounded a bit deflated, but he hadn't entirely burst her bubble. "I can't wait." She giggled, and the call ended on a chipper note, at least on Edie's end.

He rolled his eyes and tossed the phone into the seat. He cared about her, he really did, but she was so fucking pleasant that it became exhausting at times, especially when she played her games. He figured he'd go home to find she'd bought him a set of golf clubs or maybe something random like a pair of gloves. She was always doing small things for him, and while he appreciated it, it wasn't necessary.

He drove to his next meeting feeling lucky and hoping that the meeting with Wes Finkle had set a tone for the rest of the day. But when he heard the steampunk heart shift on the back floorboard, he remembered that no matter how nice and sunny the day was, he had a dark cloud looming over his head.

At the next stoplight, he looked back to make sure the sculpture wasn't messed up and stood it upright, hoping the damned thing hadn't ruined his seats. Everything looked okay.

When the light changed, he continued on, feeling a sense of paranoia creep in. What if one of his meetings was a setup? What if when he got to the location, the killer got him? No one would know what happened to him until his body turned up in a sewer somewhere, or perhaps a dump or a ditch. Being a writer, he could think of all sorts of scenarios, and not one of them had a happy ending.

15

DAREK

Darek was at the coffee pot when Max came in.

"Damn, Darek. You go away with McNamara for the weekend and come back with a rash. I'm not so sure that's a good thing." His partner was always busting his chops about Lizzy, and he made up for the weekend away from the office by doubling up on insults every Monday morning. "If that's what your neck looks like, I'd hate to see your dick."

Darek finished filing his cup. "You keep on talking, man. I bet you wouldn't say that shit if she walked in." He knew he wouldn't. Lizzy would hand him his ass, and he wouldn't do a damned thing about it.

"No, I wouldn't, and that's why I'm taking advantage of it now." He grinned wickedly. "So, tell me. Did you two get busy? I know how much you like her, and if I was going away with my hot partner for the weekend, I'd make sure I got laid."

Darek curled his lip. "Seeing that I'm your only hot partner, I'm not going anywhere with you for a weekend."

"You know what I mean, and you're avoiding the question." Max followed Darek back to his desk. When Darek sat down, Max took the opportunity to lean over his shoulder. "Well, blink twice if you boned her. I won't tell a soul."

Darek turned and blinked like a hundred times at him. "Happy?"

"Seriously?" He narrowed his eyes. "I didn't think you had. I was just kidding around."

"Does it matter? Look, I'm trying to get my shit done so I can duck out. I have to go see my dermatologist. She called me last night and asked me to come at ten."

"She? Is she hot?" Max nudged his arm.

"She's attractive."

"Who's attractive?" Lizzy's voice straightened his back, and when Darek turned around, the sight of her straightened another part of him. She had been dressed so casually through the weekend that he had almost forgotten how hot she looked dressed up for work. Her hair was up, a few tendrils framing her face, and her blouse and skirt made her look more like a naughty librarian than a special agent.

"His dermatologist," Max said. "What are you doing? Having that rash looked at? He told me you gave it to him Lizzy." Max gave a playful smirk, and Lizzy played along.

"Yeah, I pushed his ass down into some poison ivy." She gave Darek a wink and then turned to Max. "You want to know why?"

"Why is that?" Max was an idiot for playing along.

"Because he kept making stupid jokes too early in the fucking morning." She lifted her chin and dared him to say something else.

"Noted." Max turned around and faced his own desk.

When Lizzy walked away, he turned to look at Darek. "What's her fucking problem?"

Darek opened his desk drawer and got out one of his report sheets. "I'd guess it's your fucking mouth." He laughed as Max shot him the finger.

"I was just playing around." He cleared his throat. "Did you find anything while you were there, aside from a piece of ass?"

"You're really asking for it, aren't you? And for your information, no, we didn't find anything. Everything has changed down there. The landscape is way different from the reports. There are new buildings. There have been fires. You name it."

"Damn, no wonder she's in a bad mood."

"Yeah, so cut her a break." Darek was going to try and be a little more understanding about the Virginia investigation and hoped that from then on, she'd cool it a bit with the theories and focus on the new murders, which would be easier for him to control.

"Yeah, I hear you, man. I'll lay off." Max turned back to his desk, and Darek worked on finishing his report.

He got out of the office with just enough time to make it to his appointment. When Marie saw him, she had a big smile for him. She had gained a little weight since the last time he'd seen her, but it was much healthier than what she had looked like before. Darek would never forget how stressed and run down she'd looked, the fear in her eyes for her husband, and that nasty busted lip. The first time he'd seen her since high school, he'd gone on a domestic call, and there she was in her house, her lip busted from her husband, blood-stained clothes, and looking like she'd just seen the devil.

Darek hauled her husband to jail and then went back to check on her. He'd always hoped that she'd grown up and followed her dreams, and at the time, her future didn't look too bright. She'd tried to go to college, but the abuse had interrupted her education. Darek had learned that when she had invited him inside and told him all about their problems, and even though she said she wasn't ever letting him back into her life, Darek had been called out again, and that time, the beating had been even worse.

After that, he'd come around for a while, just until she was on her feet. They'd had a little romance, nothing to make the stars align, but he wasn't looking for drama in his life, which her ex had provided. By the time Darek met Megan, Marie was busy focusing on her career, which she could do once she wasn't being abused.

"You look incredible," Darek said as he walked into her office.

"Thank you; you're not so bad yourself." She waved him into the room and up onto her exam table. "Yeah, it's amazing what a little weight will do for a person, huh? I'm not a walking pile of nerves these days."

"I take it Eddie didn't come back around." He had often wondered if she'd let the man back into her life.

"Hell, no. He took off to Colorado where he hit the wrong woman. He's dead now." She gave a little laugh, and it wasn't the reaction he expected her to have.

Darek couldn't blame her, though. "Well, I'm sure that's horrible news for someone, but I can't say it's me."

"So, let's see this rash." She pulled on a pair of gloves and waited while he undid the buttons on his shirt and showed her his neck. "Oh yeah, it got you good. It looks like poison ivy. You must have come into direct contact with it when you fell. I'm surprised it didn't spread, but you might only have a mild reaction. I'll get you some stronger cream if you want, but it's already going away."

"Thanks."

"I see you still have that horrible brand." She'd never liked his mark and had only seen it a couple of times when they'd gotten more intimate years ago.

"Yeah, I wish I didn't. The things we do when we're in college, you know? It's a spring break I'll never forget because of this shit." He had always told everyone who asked the same spring break story.

"I could get rid of it for you, but then you'd just be left with another scar." She shrugged like no one would ever want that.

"Are you serious?"

"Yes, it wouldn't take a lot, actually. No more than if I had to remove a cyst, but I usually don't do unnecessary procedures." She took off her gloves and tossed them in the trash.

Darek knew he had to convince her. "Would you do it for me? If I really wanted it?"

"If you could explain to me why you want it removed, then I'd consider it."

Darek nodded. "It's simple. I'm being considered for a job at the FBI, and I feel like it's unprofessional. I see so many others who did the same crazy shit, and it's embarrassing."

"I can understand that." She reached into her pocket and pulled out her prescription pad and pen. Then she drew a football shape and put an arrow inside it. "This is how I'd cut you, taking out the unwanted flesh, and then I'd pull these two cut edges together, giving you a straight scar. You'd have a wound to tend to, but if anyone asks, you just got a cyst removed." She shrugged as she put the pad and pen away.

"How much would something like that cost me?" He wasn't going to let money get in the way and would dip into his savings if he needed.

"Considering you saved my life, I could do it for free."

"Are you sure?"

"Well, we could charge your insurance for cyst removal, but that would be fraud, so it's the least I can do for all you've done for me. If you hadn't come along in my life when you did, I'd be dead, Darek. You're a good man, and I want to help."

He needed to be reminded more than ever of some of the good he'd done, and even though no good deed could make up for the horrific ones, it was good to hear.

"I was just doing my job, but since you put it like that, when can I get this done?" He closed his shirt and started working on his buttons.

"I could see you Wednesday morning if you can be here at eight-thirty? I usually leave that window for my morning workout, but I've pulled a muscle, and it's at the point where if I don't give it a rest, *I'll* be the patient."

Darek smiled. "I'll be here. Thank you so much. You don't know how much it means to me. I really didn't think there was a way to get rid of it."

"I'll be glad to see it gone, too, and I'll do my best to give you a good cosmetic stitching to minimize the scarring."

"You're the best." He hopped off the table, and she closed the distance between them.

"I heard about your divorce." She surprised Darek with that one, and he wondered where the subject might lead. He wasn't interested in revisiting old romances and preferred his new one with Lizzy.

"Did you? Small world, I guess." He didn't realize that he and Megan had been such a big deal.

"Yeah, I heard from a friend of hers actually. She couldn't believe that Megan had stepped out on a great guy like you. I totally agree with that. I can't believe she thought that she'd do better. You've always been such a sweetheart." Her smile and mannerisms became flirtier, and he couldn't help but smile back at her.

"Yeah, I'm trying to enjoy life a bit before getting into anything too deep. I have the FBI to focus on, which would be a huge step up for me. I'm trying to behave long enough to get in, anyway." He gave her a wink and then looked at his phone.

"Well, I guess I'll see you on Wednesday morning," she said, placing her hand on his shoulder and rubbing the spot over his brand. "I'll help you put one more mistake behind you." She winked and then gave a soft laugh, and he joined her.

"That's what we seem to do for one another, fix our mistakes. That's what friends do, I suppose."

"I suppose." The way she looked him up and down, he had a feeling she'd like for them to be more than friends. He hoped he could get away before she came on any stronger.

"Thanks again, Marie." He put his phone away and headed out, wondering if she was watching him go. He couldn't wait to get back to Lizzy, especially knowing that before long, nothing was going to hold him back from her.

16

FINN

J ust as Finn got done delivering the check to Wes Finkle's, he walked out to the parking garage, which at least was a bit closer than before but still a hell of a walk when you were afraid someone was after you.

He looked around, keeping an eye out to see if anyone was around and a sharp ear to listen for footsteps.

He walked into an elevator that would take him to his level, and when the doors closed, the creaking machinery made him nervous. Instead of feeling safe, he felt trapped. All of a sudden, the thing came to a stop. Finn waited for the doors to open, and when they didn't, he started to panic.

He took out his phone and was just about to call his girlfriend, who had been MIA for hours now, when it started moving again. He put the phone away as the doors opened. He stepped out, hoping that he could still make it to his car in one piece, and something caused a sound to his right, like a garbage can being knocked over.

Before he could process what was going on, something big enough to be a person moved swiftly in his direction. He took off running as the footsteps moved closer. Finn wasn't going out in some fucking parking garage.

When he got to his car, he hurried to unlock the doors. The keys rattled as his hands shook, and he wished he'd modified the locks on the classic car to electric. He would kick himself in the pants for being frugal later. For now, there wasn't time.

He threw the door open and jumped in, locking the door and looking around to make sure the other was locked. That was when something—he wasn't sure what—cracked down on his windshield, busting it so badly that the entire thing spiderwebbed. By the time the shock wore off, the footsteps, which were running away, faded in the distance.

He sat there, shaken and in shock. He grabbed his phone and quickly dialed Bay's number.

"This better be good." Bay's voice was strained, and he was clearly out of breath. Finn's first guess was the man had just run away after smashing his windshield.

"Where are you?" Finn asked.

"Dick deep in pussy, and if you didn't have a fucking target on your back, I'd have never answered the phone."

Finn pushed the image out of his mind. That would explain the exertion in his voice. "Oh, well, I *have* had a run in with who I think is the killer."

"What do you mean?" He heard the sound of the background change, and Bay was suddenly standing outside. He was sure of it. The sounds of traffic were clearly present.

Finn's suspicion grew. "Where are you?" He didn't believe Bay for a minute. He was lying.

Bay growled as he let out a breath that sounded through the phone. "I'm standing on my fucking balcony with my cock out. Now tell me what the fuck happened or I'm hanging the fuck up."

Finn's head was swimming. "I was on my way back to my car, here in the parking garage outside of Finkle's place, and someone was waiting for me. They chased me to the car, and when I locked myself inside, they smashed my fucking windshield."

"Who was it?" The sounds changed through the phone again. Finn listened carefully, but he couldn't make out where Bay was.

"I don't know," Finn said. "He got away before I could see him. He's fast." Finn wished he had some kind of clue as to who it could have been. "I should call Darek and see if he can make a report or something."

"Are you insane? Why shine a light on yourself?"

"For one, I need a report so I can file a claim for my insurance, and for two, what if it wasn't the killer but just some asshole who's doing this to anyone and everyone?"

"Don't do it. Get your ass over here."

The sounds of sirens echoed through the parking garage. "Shit."

Bay's voice grew angrier. "What the fuck is that? Did you already call them?"

"No, someone else must have, and I can't get away. I'll just tell them I was about to call, that I'm shaken up, that won't be too hard to believe." He *was* still shaking like a leaf.

"Look, someone's calling my other line," Bay said. "If your windshield is busted, they won't let you drive, so tell them you're calling a friend for a ride, and I'll send one of my men to get you."

"Where were your men while this shit was happening?" Finn asked. Bay was supposed to have someone tailing him.

"The guy I wanted to send is tied up at the moment, but I have a feeling he'll be freed up soon enough."

Finn wondered what kind of mafia shit Bay was tied into. He always talked about his men like he was some kind of fucking gangster.

"Fine, the cop is getting out of the car." Finn hung up the phone before Bay could say anything else, and then he opened the door when the policeman knocked on his window.

"We got a report from someone who heard your window breaking. Are you okay?"

Finn stepped out of the car and shut the door. "I'm a little freaked out, but I'm not hurt. Did the person who called you see who did it?"

He hoped that at least someone had seen or heard something. Whoever the killer was, they'd taken a big risk.

"No, just that they heard it," the cop said. "The woman was so scared, she ran back inside and called us."

"Thank God she didn't get hurt." He couldn't help but wonder how much worse it could have been. Not only was he very lucky, but the woman was, too.

The cop nodded. "I'll just get your license and registration, and we'll make a report. I'll let you make arrangements for your car if you want, and I can give you a ride unless you're staying here with a friend."

"No, I was here seeing a business associate. I'm a filmmaker back in LA, and I came over to do a little legwork on that. I'll just see if he can take me where I need to go. I'm still a bit shaken."

"Yeah, I bet. This is a fine car, sir. I hate to see it like this, but if you give me a minute, I'll have you out of here."

"Thanks." Finn leaned against his car and waited. Thankfully, it didn't take too long. He got the report and hoped that his insurance would take care of the damage.

Finn pretended to go back inside and gave the policeman a minute while he waited for Bay's man to come and get him.

When he arrived, the man looked too proper to be hired, and though he seemed more like a butler or chauffeur, he wasn't going to ask the man his affiliation with Bay. The last thing Finn needed was to ask the wrong question.

He arrived at the penthouse, and when he went up, he hoped that Bay wouldn't still have company. Although if he did, it would make Bay's story more legit.

Bay opened the door and brushed his hair back as he stepped aside. "Did the police ask a lot of questions?"

"No, they think it was just some random asshole. They probably were going to mug me and smashed the car since I outran them." He hoped that was all it was.

Bay's phone rang. He answered it and growled. "Is she still at it?" Bay waited silently for the person on the other end of the line, and Finn wondered what was going on. "Did you hit her? Don't hit her. It's not going to help anything. Are you wearing gloves?"

Finn walked over to the bar and poured himself a drink, quite certain that Bay wouldn't mind.

"Put the phone on speaker," Bay said. "I want to talk to her." His temper was growing wilder by the second, and he was pacing the floor, causing the energy in the room to charge as if he were creating a power source.

Finn wondered if it was Bay's wife acting up again. She'd been known to give him trouble, and Finn couldn't help but wonder what it was like for her to be pregnant with the man's child. He couldn't see Bay as a father and wondered how fatherly he'd actually be to a kid.

"Look, you fucking bitch. I've tried to play nice. I've tried to make you see things my way, and this is the thanks I get for it? If you don't settle your ass down and stop making threats—"

Bay held the phone away from his ear, and the woman's voice on the other end of the phone screamed out so loudly that nothing he'd said was understandable.

But Bay seemed to understand her completely. "Oh? Is that so? You still don't get it, do you? I'm never going to let that happen. Don't mistake my infatuation with fucking you for safety. That's a lesson you'll learn the hard way, I'm sure."

The "fuck you" that came from the phone was audible, and the voice seemed vaguely familiar.

"Lou, take her off the speaker."

Finn was glad. He didn't need to be a party to whatever kind of abuse the man was involved in. He thought of the girl from the ritual. Emily Johnson had been her name. Bay had had the others shut her up so he could do what needed to be done, and now, Finn wondered if that was what Bay was doing. Shutting up another victim. He'd orchestrated the entire ritual when they were kids; it would stand to reason that he'd be able to orchestrate something bigger now.

Finn sipped his drink and turned to face the window. Was someone out there worse than Bay? That was hard to believe.

"Give her the injection. She'll stop her fucking screaming then. And I don't care if she bites, but you don't hit her. Do you understand me? I'll handle it." He ended the call and walked casually to the bar as if he wasn't even shaken up.

Finn was torn. The man was never going to change. "I'm heading out," Finn said. He figured if he called for a cab, then at least he'd be safe.

Bay wasn't having it. "You're not going anywhere. You've already drawn enough fucking attention to yourself."

"I didn't do anything." He couldn't believe Bay's audacity. "My fucking car is a mess. I didn't mean for anything crazy to happen. You can't just put it on me for being a victim."

"Don't raise your fucking voice to me right now. I've had enough goddamned screaming for one fucking day."

Finn could only imagine the fucking terror whoever he was knocking around was enduring, and Finn wasn't about to be a party to any more of his bullshit. He'd let Bay involve him once already, and that had haunted him for too long.

Finn had gone back into that fucking millhouse and knelt down over the girl, who someone had silenced at his request. Then Bay had given him the knife and one final command. "Do it. Show me. Make me a believer."

Finn wanted so hard to prove his love to Bay, his loyalty, but that was so long ago, and even though he craved the man now, he wasn't sure he was worth it. Bay's promises had been empty before.

"Look, I get it, okay," Finn said. "I've had a shitty day too, which is why I want to go. I'm going to get the fuck out of here, make arrangements for my windshield, which can be repaired in a matter of hours, mind you, and then I'm fucking out of here. This entire trip has sucked, and I'll do much better work at home."

Bay closed the distance between them so fast that Finn flinched. The man was in his face and close enough to kiss. "You're not going home. You owe me, and you're staying right fucking here."

17

FINN

Finn knew he better not argue with Bay since the man could strike out quicker than a snake. He went to sit on the couch, and Bay joined him.

"I can't believe you want to go home." Bay tossed back the last of his drink and turned to face Finn. "All this time wanting to be close to me, and you're still running. You're not loyal. You've stayed away for years."

"I had to live my life," Finn said. "You were living yours. It's not like we could ever really be together, as much as I would want that."

"You still haven't learned to trust me, to be my friend first, so that you might progress to be more. You've proven most difficult for me."

"Are you kidding? *I'm* difficult?" He belted a laugh and then downed his drink.

"I know you wanted to push me out, Finn. You and Logan. You talked to Hannah at that funeral about me. I heard enough from his studio to know that. That's the problem with you all. You've learned to fear this fucking killer, and you've forgotten to give me my due respect as your leader. Just like you live your lives, all coming around for one thing, my money, and only when it suits you. I think it's time you all remember who is the boss."

"You're crazy if you think we've forgotten anything that happened all those years ago, or if you think any one of them is more loyal to you than me."

"There you go, calling me crazy," Bay said. "Well maybe, just maybe I should show you how fucking crazy I am and give you another fucking test of your loyalty." He turned and took a pad and pencil from the box where he kept his coke, and then he jotted down an address.

"What's that? Are you serious? I've done everything you've ever asked."

"Here, take this. I have another job for you."

Finn had done all he could do. "I carved up some poor screaming girl for you, and I did the whole Seth thing for you. Now you have another job?" It was never going to end.

Bay sat down beside him. "You did all of that for selfish reasons, and you know it. It wasn't about me. It was about you and my money."

"That's bullshit. I didn't get paid to carve up Emily."

"You were paid with my loyalty and friendship, just like the rest of you. Every single fucking one of you owe me. You know it, and I know it. I've been the only one to offer support to you."

"You had me earn it," Finn said.

"Earn *me*, not my fucking money! Finally, for once and for all, earn *me*, Finn." His leg brushed up against Finn's, and he had the strong urge to lean in and capture Bay's lips with his. He fought the urge, knowing that he didn't want to force anything.

Finn thought he should at least hear him out. "What do I have to do?"

Bay tucked the paper into his shirt pocket and offered a sly grin. "Go there. Wait for my instruction." Bay shrugged like it was nothing, but Finn knew better.

"Does this have to do with that woman?"

"Does it fucking matter?" Bay reached out and cupped Finn's cheek. He stroked his face with his thumb, and Finn leaned into his hand, closing his eyes as he considered how much he loved the man.

"Maybe all I've ever needed is for you to want me for me, Finn. Not for my power, not for my money, but for me. The kind of loyalty I get from Mia and Lila. You've seen them with me. Tell me you don't want the same."

Finn had envied the women, but he didn't think he could fully give himself to Bay that way. To be his property, to be at his beck and call, it would take too much sacrifice. Much more than a fucking knife in some screaming girl's back.

"I'm not sure; I think I should just go home." The pressure was getting to him, and he didn't want to make a decision that would haunt him for the rest of his life, especially when he'd do it for someone who would never really reciprocate his feelings.

"That's how you want to be?" Bay stood and grabbed Finn by the arm. "Get the fuck out then. Go on. I'm done with your fucking movie, and I'm done with you."

Bay had snapped so quickly, it was completely unexpected. He'd never gotten violent with Finn, and he'd certainly not upset him this way before. "I don't want to fight, Bay."

"Yeah, you don't. So fucking leave, and forget you know me when you do. You're dead to me, Finn. Dead. You said you fucking loved me, and I've sat here believing your fucking lies for this long, but never again."

Finn couldn't believe the things he was saying, and it scared him to think of not having Bay in his life, but another part of him wanted nothing more than to run while he could. He was so torn about what to do.

He pulled away from Bay and stumbled around the coffee table, trying to get away from him. "I'm sorry, Bay. I just need time."

"That's it, run. You'll see who is in control, Finn. You'll see that you fucking need me."

Finn was so torn up that he hurried out, but he had no idea where he was going.

Once on the street, he felt like he could breathe and looked around, hoping that no one was watching him. Not the killer, not anyone. He was just about to hail a cab when his phone rang. He looked down at the screen and considered not answering Edie's call. He considered ignoring her and putting his phone away, but he needed to get the woman off his ass. "This is a bad time, Edie!"

"I'm sorry. I was just hoping you'd tell me which hotel you're in again. I think I'm at the wrong one."

He thought he might have misunderstood her. "What are you saying? Are you here? In New York City?"

"Yes, I came to surprise you, but I got to the hotel you told me you were staying at, and the girl at the counter said there's no one by your name in the hotel."

"I checked out of there, Edie. I was just about to head home, but I was chased down and nearly mugged. It's not safe here. You should have told me you were coming."

"Are you all right?" Her voice was concerned.

"Fine, I'm just not expecting you." He didn't want his life in New York to collide with his life back home. He was like two different people.

"I'm sorry, but you said you had a few days left, and I wanted to tell you the good news in person."

"Tell me now." He had forgotten about her and her surprise and hoped it wasn't something stupid that could have waited until they got home.

"No, sillykins. If I wanted to tell you on the phone, I'd have done that from California. I came to tell you in person."

"Fine. Fuck!" He hated cursing because he knew how bad Edie hated it, but dammit, her timing sucked. He had wanted time alone to think about Bay, and now he'd have to worry about her safety, too. "Look, just stay at the hotel, book a room, and we'll go up and stay the night."

"Oh, I'd love that. I'll wait for you in the lobby."

"Sounds good." He hung up the phone and hailed the taxi which brought him back to the hotel. He kept thinking of Bay the whole way there. Surely, he didn't mean everything he'd said. The man was so difficult and always asking for so much. Finn knew he wouldn't be where he was if it hadn't been for Bay's friendship all these years, and he knew he and Bay's relationship was special in comparison to the others. How could it not be?

He got to the hotel and found Edie waiting in the lobby. She jumped from the sofa, clutching her handbag as she ran into his arms. "I'm so glad you're okay. If I had only told you I was coming, maybe you wouldn't have been assaulted." She checked him over from head to toe, and he looked around, hoping no one was watching.

He patted her hands, if only to get them off of him. "I'm fine. Let's book a room, and I'll tell you all about it." He gave her a quick peck, but she planted soft kisses all over his face until he pushed her away. "Baby, I'm sore and exhausted. Could you please just book the fucking room?"

Her eyes widened. "Oh, I'm sorry, potty mouth." She frowned. "I'm just excited to see you."

"I know, baby. I'm just in a bad mood."

"Fine, any particular type of room? How about a room with a view or a nice big tub for the two of us?"

"Whatever you want. I really just want to get upstairs." He walked with her to the front desk, and while she was talking with her usual chipper language to the attendant, Finn stepped back and waited.

He looked up in time to see Raven, who was only steps away, and she had her bag of toys that he loved so much. "Hey, sexy. I hope you remembered our date." She leaned in and kissed his cheek, and he turned to see that Edie had finished at the desk and was standing wide-eyed as her lips peeled back in a scowl. As pleasant as she was normally, when she was pissed, she turned into a fucking viper.

"Who the hell is she?" Edie asked.

Raven turned her attention to Edie and her smile faded. "I'm Raven, and you are?" Finn had told her that he'd left his girlfriend back in California.

Finn was prepared to tell her the truth. "I can explain."

"Relax, honey," Raven said. "I'll share if you like, and I'll even go down on you first."

"Go *down!*" Edie looked over at Finn, her face veiled with disgust. "You've been here this whole time, sleeping with this woman?"

Raven pulled her lips in tight and held up her hands. "Look, I'm sorry, Finn, but I don't need this shit."

Edie's face was red with rage. "To think that I came here to tell you that I'm having your baby, and you've been having dirty sex with that snatch-eating harlot!"

"You're what?" Finn reached out and grabbed her arm, if only to steady himself.

"That's right, you piece of shit. I'm pregnant!"

"I *am* a piece of shit, Edie. I'm not worthy of you or a baby. I'm a horrible person, and I've done horrible things. You are right to hate me."

"All this time has been a lie," Edie said. She turned and reached down for her bag, but the bellboy who'd been listening grabbed it before he could, and like a true gentleman, took Edie by the arm and helped her to the elevator. Before the door closed, she scowled at him. "Don't ever come near me again."

The doors closed, and Finn turned to see that there was quite an audience. That was when the manager came over and asked him to leave.

He had nowhere to go and no one to turn to. He knew he had to give Edie time and hoped that she wouldn't hate him forever. He couldn't be a good father to their child even if he wanted to, so he wondered if staying away was the best thing. As he walked out of the hotel and onto the sidewalk, he looked around to figure out his next move, hoping the killer wasn't already carefully planning theirs.

At least Edie and the baby would be safe away from him, and she could go back to California and live a happy life. What options did *he* have? His life was over, his career in filmmaking was going to have to wait, and he had to call Finkle and tell him that he'd no longer need his services, certain that the man would insist on keeping the deposit.

Bay had been right. Finn did need him.

18

FINN

Finn knew that he had to get his ass back to Bay's as soon as possible. He hoped the man was still at his penthouse and not at his family home with the wife and her slutty sister.

He hailed a cab, and on the ride back, he thought about just how long Bay had been a part of his life. Finn had been one of the first Zodiacs, and he'd been there when all the rules had been made and when all of the first vows had been taken. They had all promised to take care of one another, but so far, it was only Bay who had held up that promise, taking care of the rest like it was his duty. The man had always been there, willing to help, no matter how much he seemed to hate it, and even now, while they were backed into a corner, he was standing true to the Zodiacs, making sure they were safe.

Finn knew he had to prove his love. To do whatever task Bay wanted done so that they could be together. He knew what a commitment to Bay would be. It meant being at his beck and call and catering to his whims, no matter what they were. Finn wasn't sure if he could go all the way to the dark side, but that was what it would take. He'd find the courage inside himself to kneel and be the submissive Bay wanted. He knew Bay would never be his, but if he could be Bay's, then that was enough.

Finn went up to the penthouse and knocked on the door. He wasn't the least bit surprised when Bay opened it without asking who was there. He'd no doubt seen him on his camera.

"Who are you?" Bay asked.

"I know you're upset with me, but I needed time to think." He wasn't going to tell Bay about Edie just yet, or the baby. He didn't want anything getting in the way of what he wanted.

Bay shook his head. "You always were one for doubts. But I don't have time for it anymore. Either you're with me, or you're not."

"I am. I just need you to know something. When we were young, you pulled me aside and told me you loved me, Bay. I don't think you know what it meant to me to have someone like you tell me that I was loved. I'd never heard it before. Not from my parents, not from friends. I took it to heart. I believed you."

"You have a funny way of showing it."

"Let me show you again," Finn said. "I want to do whatever you ask of me. And not for the movie. That's all done now. I'm not going to make it."

"And what about my fucking money?" Bay asked.

"I'll pay you back. Every dime. I just want to show you that I, too, love you, Bay. I've always admired you and want to have whatever it is we can have together."

"Then this should be a good test." He reached into Finn's shirt pocket and pulled out the address. "Go here. Take care of the problem for me."

"Okay, I will. I'll do it. Whatever it is." Finn knew it wasn't going to be easy, and that was okay. Life wasn't easy, and he wanted to live. The only way to be safe was with Bay. His was the best side to be on. Being alone, Finn would be dead in a week.

Bay walked him to the door, and before he let him walk through it, he turned and cupped Finn's face again. "Don't come back until it's done."

Finn met his eyes, and the intensity in Bay's cool gray eyes was sexier than any kiss could be.

Bay moved aside, and Finn left, hoping he'd make it to his task and back in one piece.

He hailed a cab, even though he hated having to get a ride, especially to someplace so important, but at least it gave him time to think about his reward.

He remembered the night he'd gotten his Zodiac brand and how he'd been the only one to cry at the pain. He'd gone to hide behind a tree and told the others he had to piss, but it had hurt so fucking bad, he couldn't hold the tears back. He stayed there for a bit longer than he should have, and Bay came across the field to join him.

"Hurt like a son of a bitch, didn't it?"

Finn nodded. "Yeah, I'm not sure I won't get in trouble when I get home. I know no one else will understand."

"Then don't show them." Bay leaned against the tree with him and placed his hand on Finn's arm.

"I know the others think I'm weak because I cried."

"Fuck them. Who gives a shit what they think? I don't think showing emotions is a sign of weakness. It's not having the balls to show them that's weak. You don't have to hide out here. If any of them crack on you about it, you tell me. I've got your back."

"Thanks, Bay. You're my best friend." He was more than that though. Finn knew it from the moment the boy had touched his arm.

"Hey, I mean it, man. As long as I'm around, nothing bad is going to happen to you. You can believe that." Bay flashed his crooked grin and took Finn's hand and gave it a squeeze. The intensity in his eyes that night had been full of conviction, and from that moment on, Finn believed in him.

He'd tried to prove to Bay how much he loved him many times since, but the most memorable was with Emily. Finn had knelt down and carved his H-shaped symbol into her back, thankful that it wasn't too complicated, remembering the words Bay had told him outside, away from all the rest. He loved him. He truly did.

Finn wanted to be worthy of that love, even now, but he hoped what he was being made to do wasn't nearly as horrible.

After paying the cabbie, he turned and walked up to the house where a big man opened the door. "Bay sent you?"

"Yeah. I'm Finn. He had something for me to take care of."

"Sounds good enough for me. Tell him thanks for sparing me the mess." The man walked out, and Finn watched him as went out to his car and drove away.

"Well, okay." He shrugged and pushed the door open. He went inside and then looked around. The house was like any other, fully-furnished and homey, with the aroma of Italian cooking wafting from the kitchen. He stuck his head in the door and saw a big pot of spaghetti on the stove. When he went over to see it up close, he noticed a small TV monitor, and on the screen, he could see someone lying on the floor, not moving.

"What the fuck?" Finn leaned in closer, but the picture quality sucked. He had to find out which room she was in, if any. Before he could make a move, Bay called his phone.

"I'm here."

"I know," Bay said. "My guy called me. He's very thankful you're there to handle things."

"What exactly am I doing? Watching this prisoner? Who is she?"

"You'll see soon enough, but it's someone who is threatening to go to the cops and snitch on us. So, you'd better take care of her before she can. She's in the basement. Try not to make a mess."

"You want me to kill her?" Finn started to panic just thinking of it. He could barely even harm the other girl, much less kill her.

"Show me, Finn. I need this done. You need this done. It's the only thing that's going to save us from being locked up like Logan. I know you like oral, but that's not all you're going to get on the inside. You do this and show your fealty to me. Do it for our love."

Those were the same words Bay had used on him back in the day, and his panic grew. "Bay." He hesitated, knowing Bay was going to be angry with him if he didn't carry out his orders, but there was no response. "Bay?"

He had already hung up.

Finn put the phone down and went down the hall. He had to find this woman and get it over with quickly. He got to the basement door and carefully went down the stairs, hoping she wasn't loose. He saw the woman lying on the floor, her dark hair a mess, and she wore scrubs.

He took a few steps, and when the floorboards creaked, she turned her head, and his heart stopped. Hannah Halston lay in the center of the room, her lips still caked with dried blood. Her eyes, though they'd been closed only a moment before, were wide and feral.

"What are you doing here?" she asked. Her voice sounded like she'd caught a cold. "You have to help me."

The plea turned his stomach. He didn't know how he could carry out what needed to be done. He didn't know what to say, but Hannah did. She got to her feet, and one foot was bloody, her sock completely coated on that foot as she limped closer. Finn could see the cuff around her ankle. He also noticed that her shirt was bloody, her pants, too.

"Bay's crazy," she said. "He caught me leaving Logan's house, and he hit me in the face." Her lip was busted, and a nasty bruise covered part of her cheek and chin. "He killed all of those people, Finn. He killed them, and he's going to kill me. He killed my brother. He'll kill you too."

Finn shook his head as she rattled on, her teeth chattering and her entire body shaking. "Please, you have to help me." She sank down to her knees in the center of the room. "Please, I know you're good. You're all good but for Bay. I see that now. You were all used, all his victims. Tad said I wasn't safe, and he knew why. He knew Bay was a monster."

Finn covered his ears. He couldn't stand to hear it. "Shut the fuck up!" he screamed.

Suddenly, he wasn't a grown man, and this wasn't Hannah Halston, Tad's sister who he'd met at Tad's funeral. No, she was Emily Johnson, pleading in that weak voice, begging for the boys to stop what they were doing and let her go. All of the same pleas: how she wouldn't tell a soul, how she would forget she was ever there, just please, please, please.

"Bay said you'd tell on us," Finn said.

"No, I won't. I promise. It's not worth it. It's not. Tell him I'll reconsider. Tell him that I'll do anything he wants, Finn. I'll be his lover, his girlfriend, anything."

Finn narrowed his eyes as his blood pumped. "He offered you those things?"

"Yes, yes." Tears streamed down her eyes. "Please tell him I've changed my mind." She was broken, completely broken.

"You're lying. If I let you go, you'll just turn us in."

She lifted her shirt. "Look what he did to me! You're not this kind of monster, Finn. You are a good boy, Tad's friend, and I'm Tad's sister."

Finn stepped closer and covered his mouth. There were two zodiac symbols carved into her flesh. Capricorn for Tad and Aquarius for Logan. Bay had marked her with each symbol.

19

DAREK

arek still couldn't believe that he'd found someone to help him remove his mark. He hadn't been so lucky in ages, and now he couldn't wait for his appointment when he could get it cut off. Having a scar was nothing. A scar could have come from anything, including a cyst which is what he was going to say he'd had removed. The best thing about it was that Marie was not only a friend who trusted his story, but she wouldn't tell a soul out of confidence. Which was perfect.

He got off work and spent the entire evening shopping for groceries and a few other things he needed around the house. He was relieved to be back home, and he'd replaced all of the groceries Megan had taken with her when she left, not that he would have eaten them anyway. He'd also replaced the toilet paper, which she'd taken, not even bothering to leave one half-used roll. It was her last way of getting the best of him, but the joke was on her. He hadn't been caught unprepared.

He even went so far as to change the sheets on the bed, just in case she'd done something to them, like let loose a venomous spider in the sheets or covered them in itching powder. He thought he'd be paranoid for the rest of his life, wondering what she'd done to the place. After the first night, he started to feel a bit safer about some things, but he still wasn't letting his guard down completely.

His phone rang while he was heating up a late dinner, and he smiled seeing Lizzy's picture on his device. "Hey, how's my favorite special agent?"

"She's wondering how her favorite detective is doing. I didn't get to see you all day, and I was wondering if that attractive doctor had stolen your heart."

"I don't know. Have you met?"

"No, why?" She giggled softly.

"Because if she had my heart, she had to take it from you." He knew it was cheesy, but he didn't care. He got to her laugh, and that was his goal.

"You're sweet. But seriously, how did it go?"

"It went good, really. She told me it's already healing, thanks to my private nurse, and I should be fine."

"Good," Lizzy said. "So how do you like being in the house again?"

"Paranoia is getting the best of me, I'm afraid."

She laughed. "That wasn't the response I thought I'd hear."

"Yeah, I can't be sure she hasn't rigged the place with boobie-traps."

"Now, why would you think that? I know she was a witch, but she played fair in the end, right?"

"If playing fair is taking all of the toilet paper with you, I suppose so." He still couldn't believe she'd stooped so low.

That made Lizzy belly laugh. "She didn't!"

"She did, but it was okay. She didn't catch me with my pants down."

"Thank heavens for that." She was laughing so hard that Darek wished he could see her. He was certain her entire face had turned red, and she was probably holding her flat tummy. She had a habit of doing that, and he thought it was funny. He'd learned all sorts of her little quirks on the road with her, and he hated to admit it, but he missed her.

"What did you do with your evening?" he asked. "Kickboxing?"

"I just finished actually, and now me and Bob are curled up on the couch. I need a shower, but I thought I'd call you before it got too late. He's giving me nasty looks for leaving him kenneled, but I wasn't going to leave him here to tear up the house."

"I'm jealous. I wish I was a cat. I'd never leave your lap."

She chuckled. "I'm glad you're not. I quite enjoyed the weekend."

"Me too. Any regrets?"

"No, not regrets, but I *am* a little concerned that we're taking things too fast and that if we're not careful, someone will find out that we slept together."

"No one will," Darek said.

"Come on. Even Max was suspicious. I saw the way he was looking at us."

"Max is an idiot, and he's not going to tell anyone, even if he is suspicious." He hoped that Max wasn't stupid enough to mention it to her like he had to him. He usually had more sense than that, which was why Darek liked him. He knew when it was okay to be an ass and when it wasn't.

"I just worry about you, is all," she said. "You'll be the one to suffer. I'm the golden child, that won't change, but Reed will be upset, and there's no telling what he'd think. Most likely that you seduced me and manipulated me into giving you a recommendation."

"He would think that? Really?"

"Yeah, I know it sounds ridiculous, but he promised Robert on his deathbed to look out for me, so he's pretty protective."

"But you're the strongest woman I know, and you're professional and not even the vulnerable type."

"Thanks, it's good to know that you get me." She giggled. As tough as she was, she was still a lady. "So, you won't mind me talking to you about the case, knowing how professional I am?"

"Not at all." Darek wondered if she had collected her thoughts on the newer evidence and stopped comparing things to the old case in Virginia.

"Well, Hannah Halston said that Tad got the brand while he was there in Virginia, but what if he got it before that and she just didn't know it?"

"It's possible," Darek said. "But who do you think would have done something like that to him?"

"His uncle, obviously. So maybe the case *does* revolve around a child sex ring. I'm not sure that Hannah didn't know more than she let on."

"She's still missing," Darek said. "Don't you think she's dead?"

"I'm not sure, but if she knew more, perhaps she was trying to create a diversion to buy the killer time, or maybe she ran off to protect herself. We should see if we can get anyone else to come forward about her. Perhaps more of her coworkers, not just her superiors."

"We could do that, but what are we going to do about Logan?" Darek asked. "He's keeping tight-lipped, hoping he's safer on the inside. I say we shake him up a bit, see if he knows anything else. Now that he's in prison, he might talk more. I don't mind going down to check him out."

"I like that idea," Lizzy said. "They know more than they're letting on. I'm afraid this body count is going to keep piling up if we don't do something. If this is some kind of pattern, and my hunch about a group is correct, there's another potential victim out there, and I think we should flush those out."

"But what if they want to remain private?" he asked. "If this is a group-related crime, none of them are going to want to come forward and put a target on their backs."

"We could offer them protection and maybe find out what kind of connection they all have. Look, Logan knew Tad, so if there are others, maybe they all know each other and have something in common."

"Or Tad and Logan were in it together?"

Lizzy let out a long sigh. "I just wish we could find Hannah again."

"I'm afraid when we do, we won't like it."

"There is no evidence of her death. Blood doesn't equal death alone. There could have been an injury."

"We're grasping at straws, and we have been since Alicia David."

"Maybe we should go back," Lizzy said. "See if she speaks to us again. I mean the evidence, of course, but you know, sometimes fresh eyes will tell us a lot, at least until someone else is killed."

"Or a lead falls into our lap, which isn't likely to happen."

"There hasn't been one shred of DNA found at the crime scenes other than the victim's, right?" she asked.

"Not a trace," Darek said. "Even the branding irons were cleaned. The killer is smart."

"And they use the same knife."

"Yes, they did." She sighed, and he wondered if she was yawning.

"We've been going back and forth for a while now; I know you're probably tired." He had a long day, too, so he couldn't blame her for being exhausted.

"I don't mind talking to you," she said, her voice soft and sexy.

"Yeah, but this is all stuff we talk about at work." Darek wanted to talk about much more.

"I know. I guess I just wanted us to take a little time off from being sneaky."

"Does it bother you?" Deep down, he was afraid she'd tell him it was a big mistake and they needed to end it before it got any worse. Or maybe he was afraid because he knew it was the smart thing to do.

"A little," she said. "I was trained to take my work seriously and not let anything get in the way of my cases. Sleeping with my partner is what Robert would have called a useless distraction."

"Ouch." Darek didn't want to be useless to her, just a distraction, a healthy one.

"I said Robert would think that, not me." She sounded a bit defensive, but then she gave a soft laugh. "I'm being ridiculous, aren't I?"

"I just wish that we could be distracted without being useless. I find you very useful." He realized how horrible that sounded as soon as it came out of his mouth. "Sorry, that was terrible."

"I don't mind it so much." Her words gave him little comfort.

"Well, I'm totally turned on by your voice, and if you were here, I'd show how much. I don't think that's useless."

"I agree. Too bad I can't come over. It's too late to go out. Besides, I'd piss Bob off. He's so content in my lap."

"I could come over; I'm sure Bob wouldn't mind." He hated to invite himself, but he was desperate and pathetic for her.

"I think we need to practice a little bit of self-control when it comes to these late-night calls."

She might exercise some restraint, but he couldn't. He'd had the biggest hard-on for her since the minute he'd answered the phone. "Are you sure?"

"Yes." She gave another yawn, and he knew he'd have to take care of things himself. "I better go before I fall asleep without my shower."

"I could come over and wash your hair for you, scrub your back. Then I could give you a nice, long massage." Nine inches of deep body massage. That was what he wanted to give her. He pushed the foul thoughts aside since they weren't helping.

"Darek, you're not being fair. Besides, I'm too sleepy, even though it sounds like heaven."

"I know, and you're not making it any easier with that sexy, sleepy voice of yours."

"Then I should really go." He could hear the smile in her voice as her tone lifted.

"Wait, how about Friday night, we come over here and have a nice dinner? I'll cook. I'm not terrible at it, I promise." He hoped they could make that a regular thing since the two of them really couldn't go out anywhere in public.

"We'll see. Sneaking around gets you maybes, I'm afraid."

"Night, Lizzy." He hated to say those words without holding her. Falling asleep with her at her home had been perfect, and he wished he could do it every day.

"Night, Darek." The phone went dead, and he pulled it away, longing for her. He finally had found something real, and there was naturally something holding them back.

He put down the phone and hoped that Friday night would work for the both of them. And even though he'd tried to ignore it, going to the cabinet for his pills and thinking about how he needed to go see his doctor for more, he couldn't cure the wild thoughts of what he wanted to do with Friday night as soon as his mark was gone. He headed to the shower and took care of his business alone, hoping all of their future conversations wouldn't end the same.

20

FINN

Finn had paced the floor, watching Hannah beg for what seemed like an hour. After a look at his phone for the hundredth time, he realized it had been forty-five minutes. He wasn't sure what he was going to do, but he knew he didn't have all night to decide.

"Please, just let me go," Hannah said. "It's that simple. Just open the door, and I'll go out and get my own help. You don't have to follow me. You don't have to get anyone's attention. I'll never tell the police anything."

"Would you shut the fuck up?" He ran up the stairs, knowing that Hannah wasn't going to be able to follow. The amount of chain she had was not enough to reach, and she had already ripped her ankle up trying to test her boundaries.

He took out his phone, not sure that Bay was going to be okay with him calling again. He had thought about the situation for nearly an hour, and he needed to find out if what she was saying was true. He couldn't believe that Bay had tortured Tad's sister. It had to be because of what she knew and not because of the relation. He finally found the courage to call Bay, and once the phone was ringing, he knew there was no turning back.

"Did you do it?" Bay asked.

"No, I haven't done it! Are you insane? This is Tad's sister, Bay. I met her at his funeral. I sat and comforted her. She's a nurse for fuck's sake, a good person, and Logan's in love with her."

"So much that he told her everything about us. I have them on tape. She's a useless slut, and she gave herself to him in order to coax him into telling."

"You didn't have to cut her up, Bay. She's bled a lot, and her ankle is ripped open and bleeding." He didn't like to see another human being suffer. It was just like with that poor girl back at camp.

"Then end her suffering," Bay said. "Make it quick, Finn. For fuck's sake, her misery is in your hands. Show her the mercy and peace of death."

"I can't. I don't know how I could possibly."

"There's a gun in the garage and knives in the kitchen. I know you can do this, Finn. Do it for us. Do it for love."

"Stop it. Love isn't like this." He thought that Bay must be sick to think the way he did.

"How do you know? You never loved me? Is there anything you wouldn't do for me?"

"Did you offer to keep her? To make her your lover?"

"Hell no," Bay said. "She's lying to you. Don't let her beat you at a game of wits, Finn. You're the smart one. She's just playing you to get you to let her go. She knows that you're having a hard time with it. Logan probably told her how weak you were. He told her everything else. Don't let her see that weakness. Do it, Finn. Do it for us, for the others who have made their lives into something. They don't deserve to go to prison because of one person running their mouth."

"I can't do it, Bay. I'm not as strong as you. You come and do it, please. Please come down here."

"You sound like a fucking coward. Just like when you were a kid. Remember when I found you standing beside that tree, Finn. I told you then that I had your back. I have your back now; I'm here. I'm here trying to make you see that this is all you have to do to have me, and then we can be together."

"I want it to be real this time, Bay." He'd longed for it to be real, for his crush to see him the same way, but he had given up hope on that years ago.

"Then show me how much you fucking love me. She's trying to ruin me, to ruin us. I tried to beg her not to turn us in, but she said she'd rather die than cut us a break. Do it, just make it fast. And when you're done, come to me, Finn. Come to me and let me prove myself to you. We can have so much if you'd only believe in me the way I believe in you, the way I've always believed in you. When no one else did. You're the most talented one of us, and the others couldn't handle it."

Finn wanted to believe in everything Bay was saying, and the fact that Bay could see into his soul, could know what he was thinking and feeling, showed that they were meant for one another. "You've always been my fantasy, Bay. Even before I knew what I wanted in life, I've always wanted to be everything to you. No one else understands you, just like no one else but you could understand me."

"I know, Finn. Do you want to know why I was always so protective of you? Why I didn't let the others come down on you, and why I didn't let them tease you for your tears? It's because you are the better half of me, Finn. You're all the good I've always wanted to be. But now, now it's time to find balance. Be as I am. Show me you have enough of me in you. You have the same courage I do. Go down there and do this for me. For our love."

"Okay, I'll do it."

"Call me when it's done, and I'll handle the rest."

The phone went dead, and Finn turned and looked at the basement door. He'd have to figure out a way to do it where she wouldn't suffer. Some way where he wouldn't have to look at her, some way where there'd be no blood, no struggle. He went to the kitchen and found a pair of gloves, and then he got a garbage bag from under the sink and carried it down.

Hannah looked at him with wide eyes. "What are you going to do with that stuff, Finn? What's Bay making you do and why?"

"You shut your mouth about him."

"You think he cares about you? He doesn't. He doesn't know what love is. He doesn't have the ability to feel. He's a sociopath, and he's got you right where he wants you. Why hasn't he come down here? Is he making you do the dirty work? Just like Lou. The big guy that was here. He had him playing the bitch. He told him all the same things."

"Shut up!" He ran over, and with his gloved hand, he struck her. Her head turned nearly around, and she fell to the floor. "You don't get to talk about him that way."

Hannah spat blood, and then he realized he'd reopened the wound on her lip. "You're just as crazy as he is." She shook her head. "You're all just as fucking crazy as him."

Finn opened the trash bag and grabbed her as she tried to crawl away. He pinned her down as he lowered himself to straddle her back. He was glad he didn't have to look her in the eyes, to see the pain of death and loss as he'd seen before at Tad's funeral, and how that death and loss was now her own. He wrapped the plastic over her face, pulling it tight as she struggled, but as if she knew it was her time, she stopped struggling, and after what seemed like ten minutes, he moved off of her. But it wasn't as long as it felt. It couldn't have been because she jerked on the floor. He threw his knee into her back and pushed her down hard. Her neck made a sharp cracking sound, and then Hannah went limp.

It was done.

Finn didn't move, this time taking a minute to make sure she wasn't going to wake up. She was quiet. The screaming, the breathing and panting, it was all quiet now.

He rolled off her and backed away across the floor, scrambling to get as far from her as he possibly could.

He looked at Hannah who was lying still, her neck in a twisted position, and he felt the sting of bile at the back of his throat. He tried hard to hold it down, but he threw up in the corner against the wall. It took a minute to get his breath after.

Finn was suddenly aware that he was alone, and he quickly pulled out his phone and dialed Bay's number. When he heard the soft hello from him, Finn burst into tears. "It's done."

"Good job. I'm proud of you, Finn. You've shown me you really love me, don't you?"

"Yes, I do. I really do."

"I know. Listen to me, Finn. I need you to wait for Lou. And when he comes back, the two of you will take care of her. You'll put her someplace where no one will ever find her, and if they do, don't worry. They'll think the killer did it, not you."

"And we'll be together, you and me?" Finn was still waiting for the other shoe to drop, for Bay to tell him it had all been a joke, and he'd fallen for it. But instead, Hannah had been wrong.

"Of course. You're mine, Finn. You've always been mine, though."

"I love you."

"And I love you, Finn. I always have." His voice was so soft and sincere that Finn believed every single word. He had no reason not to. Things were just as Bay had said they would be, and he'd never heard Bay use such sweet and tender tones with anyone, not even Mia or Lila.

More tears streamed down his cheeks, and he wiped them away. "I need to clean up a bit, but I'll be ready for Lou." He had to get himself together, and he tried to control his breathing so Bay wouldn't know how hard he'd been crying. But Bay never said a word about tears.

"Good, I'm glad you're okay, Finn. I was worried you wouldn't do it for me, but I am so glad I was wrong. You've made me so proud." Bay's encouragement had been amazing, but his praise was better than anything in the world. Finn's every fantasy was going to come true.

They ended the call, but Bay assured him he could call back if he needed to and that made Finn feel even better. He tried not to look at Hannah as he walked around her to get the cleaning supplies. Then he mopped up his vomit. He didn't bother with Hannah and the mess of blood she'd left around the room in the past few days. That was to be expected, but he wouldn't let Lou show up and see his weakness, for fear that he'd tell Bay.

He went to the bathroom to take a piss, and when he washed his hands, he saw himself in the mirror. He was a mess. His long blond hair had been drenched with sweat and tears, especially the one unruly strand that hung down in his eyes. His clothes were wrinkled, and there was a little stain of blood on his pants, which was barely visible.

He wasn't worried about a thing, not getting caught, not going to prison. Bay would never let that happen. As for the crime, he couldn't believe he'd done it, and the wild look in his eyes showed him that he was stronger than he'd expected. He took a deep breath and pushed aside any remaining tears, and he sought comfort in the fact that the grisly work was done. Now, he was going to get everything he wanted.

21

DAREK

The sound of Lizzy's voice brought Darek's head around, and just as he was about to say good morning and let her know about his appointment, he noticed she was on the phone. "I'm with my partner now; we'll be down in about twenty."

She ended the call and spun around to face him, the anger on her face filling him with concern.

"What was that all about, and where are we going?" Darek asked.

"Hannah Halston has been found."

Darek had waited a week to hear that news. He had thought that his partner's reaction would be much different than anger. "Is she alive?"

"No, she's not."

"Let me guess, stabbed and cut up?" He winced thinking about Hannah being torn apart like the others.

"Not this time. The first on the scene said the only wound they could see was on her ankle, though she was covered with blood. Officer Coleman said it looked like she'd been tied up."

"So, now our killer is a kidnapper? Interesting." It wasn't common for a killer's style to change, but it wasn't unheard of.

Lizzy tucked her phone into her blazer. "I'm not sure, but we need to get down there. She was found in the water, down by the pier."

"The same pier where Victor Barnes was found?" The same one he used to frequent himself when shit was bad with Megan.

"Yeah, that's the one. So far, that's the only fucking thing that's consistent." Lizzy shook her head in disgust and leaned against his desk.

Darek reached out to comfort her, putting his hand on hers, which was right in front of him on the desk, but she pulled it away. He looked around and wondered if anyone was watching, but there wasn't anyone else around, not even Max.

"Is everything okay?" he asked. "I haven't seen you have this reaction before."

Lizzy smoothed her hair back. "I just don't understand, I guess. She was a nurse and had been through so much."

"Yeah, and let's not forget the fact that Logan Miller has been locked up. He's not likely responsible unless she was dumped before he was hauled in." Darek thought that now he'd be free and a much easier target.

"So, we'll have to let him go unless he really *did* kill Lidia Hobbs." Lizzy didn't seem any more convinced of that than Darek, which was not at all.

"We both know he didn't," Darek said. "I've seen reactions before, and his wasn't that of a person who had killed the woman who was taking care of him. It just didn't make sense."

"Come on, we better hurry. I told him twenty minutes." She pushed off his desk, and he got up to follow her.

They got in his car, and once Lizzy was buckled in, he reached over and put his hand on her knee. "Are we okay?"

"We're fine, but we're also at work, and I have to focus on this case." Her tone was a lot sharper than he'd expected, and he drew back his hand and gripped the wheel.

"Noted." He started the car and drove them down to the scene where a few homeless men stood watching the first responders.

Officer Coleman was still on the scene, and Darek walked over to join him while Lizzy went straight for the body, which was already in the ambulance. "Is this where she was found?" he asked.

Coleman nodded. "Yeah, there was no trace of her phone or ID, but I remembered her coming into the station. I think everyone remembers her. She was so willing to speak about her brother's innocence. It looks like someone was eager to shut her up."

Darek agreed with the officer's assessment. "Any idea how they did it?"

"I told Lizzy about her ankle on the phone. It's pretty gnawed up. Looks like she was tied up for a while. There were bruises and lacerations. I didn't see anything else, just bloody clothes and what this nasty water didn't wash away. If I had to venture a guess, I'd say she was either drowned or suffocated."

"Well, we'll get her down to Dr. Cobb's office, and I'll let you know if you're right or not. I wouldn't go taking any bets, though. She could have been drugged or poisoned. This killer is certainly trying to send a fucking message this time." He checked his phone, knowing he couldn't stay, and as soon as he got a moment free, he was going to have to call Bay and tell him what happened.

"Good luck with this one," Coleman said. "I hope you find the answers soon. Before we're fishing another pretty girl out of the river."

Darek patted Coleman on the back and then went to check on Lizzy. She was standing over the body of Hannah Halston, which has a bluish tint but not nearly enough bloat to indicate she'd been there any length of time. "It looks like it was a fresh dump. She's in pretty good shape considering."

Lizzy sighed. "Yeah, it could only have been done a couple of hours ago at best. Probably before the sun came up." She turned to one of the officers from the forensic team who had been on the phone when Darek walked up. "I want the boys processing the area, combing for any clues, especially anything that could have been used to suffocate her, and get those homeless men rounded up for questioning. They had to have seen something." Lizzy's voice was commanding, and she was in a take-charge mood that she seemed to reserve for work alone. It was sexy, but very much like she was a different person when she was in this mode. He liked the softer side, the side that curled up to him between the sheets.

"Yes, ma'am." The officer, who Darek thought was named Kenny, walked over to the edge of the pier to talk to Coleman.

"Whoever did this, they didn't weigh her down at all," Lizzy said. "Usually, if someone is kept, which her ankle seems to indicate, they take the time to weigh the body before a water dump because they have the time to do it and those bodies aren't found as quickly. This was a rushed killing. Someone was probably desperate, eager to get rid of the body, to distance themselves from the corpse, perhaps. I think that's why they smothered her. No blood on their hands. I want to get Dr. Cobb on the phone. I'm following her to his office."

"Yeah, about that," Darek said. "As much as I want to stay with you and get my hands dirty, I have an important appointment with the dermatologist." He couldn't believe the timing, but he didn't want to miss his chance to lose the incriminating mark. He looked at the time, and he needed to get there within the next twenty minutes, or he'd be late.

"Seriously? Can't you reschedule? It has to be this morning?" The anger was really set in her brow now, and he considered cancelling the procedure so she wouldn't be pissed off at him.

Seeing Hannah's body between them made him feel even more like shit. She was Tad's sister, the one he was supposed to have helped look after, but if he didn't get that fucking brand removed from his shoulder, he could have a shadow of suspicion on him, and that wouldn't fucking do anything to help his relationship with Lizzy, either.

"I wish it could, Lizzy, but I have a cyst that's getting removed. I can't put it off. I'm due in like twenty, and if I go right now, I can still make it. I only came by the office to let you know. Then this grabbed my attention."

He'd wondered what her reaction would be, and his first guess was correct. She was pissed.

"I thought everything was fine the other day, Darek? You lied to me. Are you sure it's not something more serious?" Her eyes were still hard and not at all filled with the kind of concern she was expressing verbally.

"I didn't lie. You asked how it went and I told you." He didn't deliberately leave out the cyst story but hadn't told her because it wasn't true.

"Fine, go see your lady dermatologist while I process this crime scene and talk to Dr. Cobb about a woman who has been missing, who happens to be the sister of the person we pinned three murders on." She turned her back to him and walked over to Kenny, leaving Darek alone with Hannah.

He looked down and thought of Tad, his pleading in those final minutes, his determination. He had asked Darek to look after her, and he had failed. Now, it was time to protect himself. He walked off without another word and headed to his car. If he left now, he'd still make it in time.

Once he got on the road, he picked up his phone, and it rang in his hand. He was going to call Bay, but it seems that Lizzy was calling him.

"Yeah?" he answered.

"You're really leaving me here to deal with this shit alone?"

"You said you're riding in with Hannah. I didn't think you needed a ride."

"That's not my point. I need you to be here, to look at the evidence with me. Call your doctor and cancel the procedure. I'm just thinking you really should be here in case Reed asks how you're doing on the case. You know I have to meet with him later."

"I'd think that you would cover for me and that he'd understand I have a doctor's appointment." Darek slowed the car and took the next exit. He still had seven minutes, and it was going to take every single one of them to make it on time.

"This is the fucking FBI we're talking about. Your cases come first."

"I can't, Lizzy. It's something that needs attention, and I'm dealing with it as soon as possible, which is this morning. I can't help it if

Hannah showed up. I can't cancel. I already asked for a favor to get this taken care of right away."

"How long will you be?" Her tone had softened a bit but not much.

"An hour. Maybe a little longer." He checked the clock and knew he was going to have to call Marie, apologize, and let her know he was still on his way. "I swear, this isn't going to take all fucking day."

"Okay, fine. I just want you to get a report, and I don't want to have given my recommendation if this job isn't important to you."

"How can you say that? You know this is important to me. You're important to me, too, Lizzy."

"I know. I'm sorry I freaked out. I just don't want anything to hinder you, you know?"

Darek felt a sense of relief that she was not upset with him. He could understand her wanting him to succeed and be accepted, especially since she'd put her neck out for him. She was so passionate about her work, and he loved that about her.

When their call ended, he tried to ring Bay, but it was no use. The man apparently wasn't going to answer his phone. He'd have to tell him later. He called Marie and made sure she was ready for him, and she told him not to worry about a few minutes.

He pulled into the garage of the medical center, and after finding himself a place to park, he took a deep breath before going inside. He traced the arrow-shaped Sagittarius brand with his finger and was glad that he was about to officially be out of the Zodiacs for good.

22

FINN

Despite the fact that he'd gone with Lou, who showed up just after midnight, the two had more problems than he cared to relive.

Lou had backed the car into the garage, and while Finn hadn't wanted to move the body, the older man insisted. They waited for what seemed like forever for Bay to tell them the location he wanted her dumped and that they were supposed to weigh the body down.

The bag of concrete Bay told them to use wasn't in the garage, and because of the hour, they couldn't just go out and buy some.

"What are we supposed to do?" Finn asked.

"Fuck it, it doesn't matter," Lou said. "You know as well as I do, ain't no one going to find this body if we tie her up with bricks."

Finn had felt like the bricks would never stay, and sure enough, when they'd gone down to the pier where Bay had said to dump her, there were too many people around. They left and drove around for what seemed like an hour, until even Lou started getting paranoid.

Lou had taken the first chance and stopped next to the pier, where he jumped out and yelled at Finn to help. "You're going to make a lousy hit man," he said with his phlegmy voice.

Finn ignored the comment and helped him toss Hannah in the

river. Before anyone could see, they jumped in the car and sped away, Finn barely closing his door before the car jerked him back in his seat and the motion swung it toward him.

Lou had dropped him off a block away from the penthouse. "This is as close as I get," he said. Then he drove away as Finn got out and headed upstairs.

Bay was gone, most likely at home, snuggled into his bed with his wife and her sister.

Finn had laid down and closed his eyes, and that was the last thing he remembered.

He lay in Bay's bed, the sun shining in the window casting beams across his chest, and he lifted his hand in the ray to see if he was still real. He didn't feel real; he didn't feel like anything or feel anything. There was an overwhelming numbness, one that had crept in somewhere in the middle of the night when he realized he had to touch Hannah's dead body.

He'd done that to her, made her limp and lifeless, at least until it was time to pull her out of the trunk. By then, she'd gone rigid, her body stiff with rigor mortis, and it almost made him lose whatever was left in his stomach. He had managed to keep it down, which was good since Lou seemed to hate him. No need to give the man another reason.

He got out of bed and wondered if the world outside had already learned of what he'd done. If those men, the ones he hadn't seen until they were speeding away, had found what they had left behind.

He could still hear the body hitting the water and figured if he couldn't get it out of his head, those men were liable to have heard it, too. He looked out the window, noticing that the day seemed normal, busy traffic, lots of people. Just your average Wednesday. Except today, he woke up a killer.

The phone rang in the room, and it nearly made him jump out of his skin. He wasn't sure if he should pick it up, so he let it ring. He looked at his phone and found it lying on the floor. He picked it up. Dead as Hannah.

He looked for a charger, trying to push the thoughts from his mind. The overwhelming guilt and the misery were not going to escape him anytime soon. He didn't know if he could bear it. He needed Bay. He needed the other man to tell him that things were going to be okay.

He remembered being younger, being shipped off to camp by two parents who couldn't wait to get rid of him. The long hours they worked weren't enough, and they needed several hundred miles more between them. He remembered that loneliness, the feeling of being alone in a crowd, and how writing and reading had taken him away from it all.

He didn't need an escape other than books, but his father thought he'd be better off on a real-life adventure, and boy, had he gotten one.

Those first days at camp were brutal, but once he'd met Bay, it all changed. He actually forgave his parents, who he'd realized weren't much different than other parents trying to make it in the world.

He wondered what they'd think of him now. They hadn't been in touch for a long time, but neither had he. He'd taken up filmmaking, and they'd begrudgingly let him have his college money, even though they'd wanted him to be a doctor or a lawyer, something "realistic," as his father would say.

He hadn't earned their respect until he started making his own way and sold scripts, but he knew if they could see him now, they'd disown him and call him a disgrace.

He went to the shower, and after turning it on, he stepped inside, not caring what temperature the water was. He didn't deserve comfort, but he was so numb, not even cold water could bring him around.

Sitting on the floor, he curled himself into a fetal position, his knees to his chin, and closed his eyes, but every time he did, the image of Hannah's lifeless body was all he could see.

He thought of how much Tad would hate him and how much Logan would want to kill him. But he'd done it for all of them, for their secret, to keep them from a shameful legacy that would never let Logan see freedom again. Logan had trusted her, and just as Bay had said, she'd used him, lured him into telling their secrets, knowing how weak and vulnerable he'd been.

But no matter how much Finn tried to convince himself, he couldn't believe he'd done the world a favor.

He finally picked himself up and lathered his body, letting Bay's scent, his delicious, fresh-scented soap cleanse him. His tears flowed, and he knew that once he stepped out of that shower, he wouldn't cry again. At least, not in front of Bay. He couldn't appear weak to him anymore.

When he turned off the water, he heard footsteps in the next room, and as he stepped out of the shower, Bay walked into the bathroom.

"There you are. How are you holding up? I've been trying to call you all goddamned morning."

"My phone is dead." Finn turned to the sink and found his tooth-brush, which thankfully, along with all of his other belongings, had been left in the room.

"That's why I called the landline. If you had bothered to check the caller ID, I wouldn't have had to come down here and make sure you're okay."

"Scared I hung myself with one of your neckties?" He couldn't say the thought hadn't crossed his mind in the past twelve hours.

"If you want to hang yourself, use something that's a bit longer and do it from the balcony. I don't want any stains on my rugs." He gave Finn his devilish grin and then walked out, leaving him to brush his teeth.

When Finn finished his morning rituals and found something comfortable to put on, he joined Bay in the front room. He stood near the bar, looking at his phone.

"Lou called and said your first body dump should be your last."

"I wasn't aware I was in training, Bay." His tone was sharp, but he didn't care. He didn't have the strength needed to kiss the man's ass.

"Careful with the tone, Finn. I'll think you don't like me."

"Maybe I don't right now. No one has to like you all the time, Bay. You can be a real asshole."

"And yet, you have a major crush on me. What does that say about you?" He stared dead into his eyes and Finn cringed.

"I can't believe I did it. I let you talk me into it."

"You did it because you wanted to get what you want from me, my admiration. That's not my problem, friend. It's yours."

"Well, what happens now? I've proven myself to you. I've done what you asked."

"And I appreciate it. You proved your love and fealty. Good job."

"Is that all you have to say to me? Good fucking job? We had a deal." Finn felt the cold sting of betrayal, knowing Bay was doing the same thing he always did, making promises he had never intended to keep. "This is just like before. Just like when you had us hurt Emily Johnson for your stupid ritual. All because some fucking nanny of yours told you it would give us strength and make us powerful."

"Watch what you say about her." Bay's eyes lit with fiery hatred. He had always been so protective of his nanny, even when the boys were younger and Finn wondered what kind of connection the two actually had.

Bay had told them that she'd done spells and taught him everything he knew about the zodiac and how the signs influenced everything. Bay had always spoken with such a passion for those things that it was easy to be convinced that he was right. He had certainly charmed the others as much as Finn and used whatever he could to get them all together to do the ritual. Finn was ashamed for trusting him now that the reality of what he'd done sank in.

"You used that bullshit on me when we were kids, and I listened, just like last night. Even though it's haunted me since. Everything Hannah said was true. You were just trying to get your way without getting your hands dirty." He felt his heart breaking as the adrenaline pumped so hard through his veins, his hands turned cold.

"If you don't settle yourself down, you'll see just how much I like to get my hands dirty. Do you think the word of some meddling bitch is better than mine? Then I suggest you go fish her stiff ass out of the fucking river and see what she can do for you. Or you can show me some fucking respect, and maybe I'll allow you to stay with me as promised."

He had never seen Bay so livid. He was shaking, and from what he knew about the man, not much had ever rattled him in that manner. It chilled Finn to the bone.

"Tell me you're going to hold up your end of the bargain." Finn knew he was only going to piss Bay off more, but he needed to hear him say it.

"Yes. It is my intention, but you tell me, Finn, do you still trust me? Do you still want to do anything and everything for me?"

He considered those words carefully. He had a life back home, and he knew he needed to get to it, but knowing that he and Bay had a bond, something special between them, was so appealing that he would consider a move once things settled down.

Finn looked at his only crush, whose attractiveness made him ache. As much as he wanted to deny him, he had already done the terrible deed and sealed the deal. He may as well reap the rewards. "Of course, I do, Bay."

Bay walked over to the closest chair and lowered himself to sit. He palmed his drink and took a sip. Then, he patted his knee. "Come to me. Show me how serious you are."

This was the moment Finn had been waiting ages for. He'd lusted after the man for so long, holding out hope that one day he'd get to this point. He took a few steps forward, then dropped to his knees and crawled across the room until he rested his head on Bay's knee.

"I'd do anything for you," Finn said.

Bay patted his head. "Don't worry. That's what I'm counting on."

23

DAREK

Darek arrived at Marie's office two minutes late, but thankfully, she understood his job was a bit unpredictable.

"I'm surprised you made it in at all," she said. "I would have understood if you needed to reschedule."

"I didn't want to do that. I really appreciate the favor, Marie."

"I'm a bit behind myself. I didn't call any of my assistants in to help me, and I'm afraid that I've still got to set up all of the supplies, get the instruments ready, find my numbing agent, and diagram the procedure."

"Then I don't feel so bad."

"It will only take me about fifteen minutes, give or take, so come on back and relax a bit while I get to work." She was dressed in a sexy blouse, and he wondered if she'd worn it for him until she stopped by her desk and pulled on her long, white coat before leading him to the same room he'd been in before.

"Have a seat on the table, and I'll be right with you." She went to work gathering what was needed out of drawers and cabinets and put them out on a tiny tray.

He fidgeted with his phone and sent Lizzy a text. *About to go under the knife. Wish me luck.*

She responded immediately. *Luck! I hope it goes well, need you here.*

He had put her in a bad place. He hoped he'd make it out in time to grab lunch with Lizzy and go over what she'd learned.

Marie put a hypodermic needle on the tray and a vial of medicine. "I'm almost done, I promise. I am second-guessing not asking one of my girls to come in early, but they look forward to the late start, and I knew you wanted to keep it private. Besides, I have you all to myself." She chuckled softly. "Are you having a good morning?"

"I've had better, but it's okay. All part of the job."

"Oh no. Tough start, huh?"

"Yeah, a recent missing person was dragged from the river. Nothing new." He had seen it so many times, but never anyone he had this kind of relation to.

"Wow, the evil in this world. I tell you, it gets worse every single day." She shook her head. "Well, I hope that once this is done, you have a much better finish than your start."

"Me too."

"Okay, Darek. To begin, I'm going to give you some numbing. This should take effect pretty quickly, so once we get started, the procedure shouldn't take me very long. I just want to draw some guidelines to make sure I'm making the best possible cuts to ensure not only a clean scar but to completely rid you of this lame act of rebellion." She giggled, and Darek tried not to move as he chuckled under his breath.

She took a black-tipped pen and started at the tip of his arrow to the end of the shaft, drawing the same football-shaped pattern she had on paper. "That's going to do nicely, and I won't have to take away any unwanted skin."

"I'd appreciate that. Is this going to be tough healing process?" He hoped he wasn't going to have to doctor the thing a lot or change a ton of bandages.

"No, sir. You just keep it clean, change the bandage when needed." She made it sound like a snap.

He wasn't happy that the needle looked so long, and he wondered just how numb she was going to make him as she stuck him repeatedly along the drawing, each time deadening the area a little more.

"Why all the sticks?" he asked. She could hurry up and get that part over with, and he'd be a hell of a lot happier.

"I want you good and numb. Don't worry. I'm almost done." She chuckled. "If you hate the needle, just wait until I get my scalpel."

He didn't want to tell her how relieved he'd be once that part was over too, and not just because he didn't want to be carved up. It seemed like a dream come true to be losing the fucking brand once and for all.

"Okay, so while this is healing, you need to be careful that you don't rip your stitches by doing anything too physical, and by that, I mean tackling bad guys."

He wanted to ask her if sex was okay, but he figured that she would take it as an invitation. She'd given him the eye so many times, he was surprised she could see what she was doing.

She reached for her scalpel. "Okay, let's get this rolling. If at any time you feel anything sharp, you let me know. You might feel a bit of pressure. That's normal. No stinging pain, though."

He turned his head and didn't watch. He never felt anything. He was surprised when a moment later, she put something down on the tray, and he made the mistake of turning to look. It was surreal to see a part of him he thought he'd never lose lying on the table. The little piece of bloody flesh was worth losing if it meant he couldn't be physically connected to the other Zodiacs. And best of all, he couldn't wait to be with Lizzy. To have her run her hand over his body, to see him shirtless in the morning after a long night of passion.

"Okay, let's stop this bleeding." He listened as she cauterized the wound, making a wet sizzling sound. "Okay, let's get you closed up."

"That's it? You're done?" It really wasn't so bad and a lot less painful than what Logan had done. No blow torches for him.

"Well, the stitching is going to take a minute, but yes. I want to make sure I make a good stitch so you will still be wearing those tank tops like you used to in high school. All those rippling muscles, they deserve to be seen." She looked up, giving him a devilish smile.

"I haven't worn sleeveless in a long time."

"Back in the day, that's all you wore. I liked it. I always wondered if your mother hated what you were doing to your shirts, but I was glad she allowed it."

He hadn't known Marie had paid that much attention to him back then. "She didn't care."

"How's she doing?"

"Alzheimer's is taking its toll," he said. "There isn't a whole lot I can do but sit and wait for her to forget what little she remembers."

"Do you see her often?" She went to work with the sutures, the little, curved needle sewing him up like he was made of cloth.

"She's in a nursing facility. It's better that way now that my father is gone. I can't take care of her and work, so it's a good option. She gets great care, and they can look after her twenty-four-seven."

"That's good. Some people hate those places, but they are life-savers for people who can't convalesce their parents full time."

She gave him three stitches inside and seven out and finally sewed the final stitch. "Okay, you're done. Now, you just have to come back in about a week so I can remove your stitches." She patted him on the back.

"Could I do that myself? I did it once when I was younger." He had taken out his friend's stitches at a party. It wasn't more than a few snips and a tug, and they'd gone back to drinking. He knew he could handle it now, especially sober.

"Well, you could, but then I couldn't see you again. Unless you'd like to come to my place and let me take them out there, and after, I could make you dinner." Her eyes were hopeful when they met his, and he knew he'd have to let her down easy. Thankfully, she'd already done the procedure.

"I would, but I'm seeing someone." If he hadn't started something with Lizzy, he would have taken her up on the offer.

"Oh, I didn't think you'd start dating this soon after the divorce. I'd hoped I'd beaten the other ladies to the punch." She seemed disappointed, but not to the point of awkwardness, which was a relief.

"Well, it's new. We're not committed, but I'm trying to be good to her, and I know she wouldn't like me having dinner with anyone else."

"Well, I tell you what, since I was late to the party, how about you just keep me in mind in case something doesn't work out?"

"Will do, Marie. Do you still need to see me about the stitches?" He gave her a sidelong look, and she shook her head, a bright smile on her face.

"Feel free to take them out yourself." She gave him a wink. He really liked her and was glad she seemed okay with the rekection. He only hoped she didn't send him a bill.

They shared a laugh, and then she finished up writing him a prescription for pain meds. Then he was on his way.

He looked at the time and realized that despite how fast she'd been, he had still taken an hour longer than he'd expected to, and it was just after eleven. He tried to call Lizzy, but she didn't respond. By the time he got his prescription and grabbed a bite of lunch so he could start his medication, it was after one.

She would no doubt go on with her day without him.

He pulled up to the station and hoped that Max was around to tell him what he'd heard. But when he went into the office, there wasn't anyone around. He called Lizzy, hoping this time she'd answer.

She did. "What do you want, Darek? I'm about to go inside and have my meeting with Reed." Her voice was quiet, and he heard other men talking in the room.

"Did you talk to Dr. Cobb?" He sat at his desk and kicked back, his head spinning from his medication.

"Yes, but I can't talk about that right now. I have to go in."

"Call me as soon as you're out?"

"Yeah." The phone went dead, and he wished he could slam his down. Broken screens had taken all the joy from that stress release.

Max walked in, and Darek could barely move for fear the room would spin.

"Damn, man, you look like you're about to hurl," Max said.

"I feel like it. I think the pain meds from my procedure this morning are making me sick."

"Damn. You already missed all the fun, I heard."

"Lizzy said something about me missing work?" Darek asked.

"I went with her in your place. So yeah, I got an earful."

"You went along? So, what's the verdict? Did you find out a cause of death? Was there enough time to do a preliminary?" His head was swimming, and he closed his eyes, hoping it would help.

"Not determined, but Dr. Cobb is going to call us as soon as he can get to it. He had his assistant on it while we were there, but he had to leave for an exam."

"I bet Lizzy lost her shit over that one since I'd had something else going on, too."

"Yeah, she's a little miffed over that, but she's worried about you. She kept asking me if it really was a cyst and what I knew about it. She said she was scared you were hiding something serious. Of course, when I asked her why she cared so much, she told me to mind my own fucking business. So, maybe you can make it up to her in private." He grinned big just as Darek jumped from his seat and lost his lunch in his wastebasket.

"I'll get the janitor. You should go home, my friend."

Knowing Max was right, Darek got to his feet and grabbed his keys.

Max snatched them out of his hands. "Not so fast, buddy. I'll drive."

24

DAREK

Waking up with a sore shoulder was still better than waking up with a Sagittarius symbol burned into his arm, but he wasn't quite expecting to hear the frantic knocking on his door.

He rolled over, feeling much better, and got to his feet. He didn't bother with a robe and went directly to the door in his shorts.

"Yeah?" He threw the door open, and Lizzy stood there with her fist raised, about to give the door more hell.

"Hey, sleepyhead. I came to check on you and see if you're going to be around this morning."

"I figured you were still mad at me. You never called." He pushed the door open and stepped back to invite her in.

She hesitated a moment but then went inside. "I was upset, but my meeting ran late, and then Max told me that you had gone home sick."

Darek led her into the kitchen and warmed up the coffee pot before adding water. "Yeah, I had to get different pain medication. Turns out the other didn't mix well with my daily meds. I'm good now."

"Good." She looked at his shoulder and winced at the bandage. "Wow, it's a bit bigger than I thought. Let me see."

He uncovered it, knowing he had to change his bandage for the day, and her eyes widened. "What's that, like two inches? It must have been a nice little cyst. Did they biopsy?"

He grabbed two mugs from the rack. "It wasn't anything dangerous, but yeah, it's about two and a half. Does it make me look tough?"

"Maybe if it were on your face or neck. You know how those neck tats make people look like serial killers?"

"Right? Dammit and there I was hoping." He liked playing with her and loved to make her laugh.

The coffee maker spat out the first cup, and he passed it off to her and then prepared another.

"Thanks," she said before taking a sip.

He wanted coffee with her in his house every morning or at least most. It was definitely something he could get used to. "You're welcome. So, did Dr. Cobb ever find out anything?"

He knew the man would call her with any information he had anytime, day or night, and he'd found out about her night trips to the ME office.

"I talked to him last night, actually. He found two carvings on her stomach, and both were zodiac symbols."

Darek shook his head. "You hadn't seen them when you and Max were there?"

"No, I had been so focused on the ankle, and they hadn't even undressed the body. But I went back last night after Cobb called, and sure enough, they are Capricorn and Aquarius."

"No others?"

"Nope. Someone broke her neck, but there were signs of lack of oxygen. He found a small piece of plastic in her teeth, and he thinks that's what was used. She'd tried to bite her way through and probably succeeded, but then he thinks that just pissed the killer off. They jerked at whatever was around her face, causing some bruising, and then snapped her neck. Dr. Cobb said she lay on her stomach for hours after her death. Lividity was increased in the front part of her body."

"And what about the ankle?" Darek asked. "Did you figure out what was used?"

"It appears that she was kept chained with a metal cuff around her ankle." It was hard to think Lizzy was talking about Hannah Halston. Darek still couldn't believe how crazy things had gotten; how out of hand.

"It's nothing like the killer's MO," Darek said.

"No kidding, and if this was anyone but Hannah, I'd say we had a copycat on our hands. The symbols are interesting because they are the two symbols she'd have been aware of."

Darek nodded. "Yeah, most people don't know what the symbols look like. I'm sure Hannah didn't, either."

"Right, but she knew Capricorn because her brother had it, and Logan's sign was Aquarius, which we can only assume she saw at least while they were having sex."

"You think she did them to herself?"

"They were at a strange angle. She could have totally carved them on herself. They also weren't too deep, although still crazy enough to hurt. I don't know how she did it, but I think she wanted us to know that it's all connected."

"That's a good theory, and it's smart she did that."

"She was a smart woman," Lizzy said. "She was sending us a message for sure, but we have to figure out who took her and who killed her and why. I'm not convinced it's the same person."

"Maybe there is more than one killer?" Darek asked.

"It would make sense. A couple of homeless men saw two men in a black car about four-thirty that morning, which is when we think her body was put there."

Darek didn't like the thoughts he was having and wondered if Bay had anything to do with Hannah's death. Had he done it to shut her up and then gave her symbols to make it look connected? He had his own theories but could never tell Lizzy.

Lizzy shrugged. "Anyway, I wanted to tell you all about it and that

I'll be the one playing hooky today. Reed wants me on a side project, but it shouldn't take much time."

"So, I won't get to hang out with you all day?"

"At least not some days, but I'm still on this full time. There's just something from an old cold case that he wants me to look over. You know those are my favorite." She stepped closer, and he pulled her into his arms, hoping it was okay and glad she wasn't angry with him. "So, I wanted to tell you I'm sorry for being upset yesterday. I know things are going to pull us away, and I can't blame you for wanting your cyst removed. I'm glad you're okay."

She searched his eyes, and then they kissed, long and deep. He didn't want to let her go when she pulled away, and he seriously thought about picking her up and carrying her to his bed.

"It's okay as long as you're not still upset with me," he said. "I really just wanted the thing gone before I got my promotion."

"I like your confidence, and I thought I'd let you know that Reed asked me a few more questions about you. Nothing I can tell you, but I put in another good word." She gave him another quick kiss on the lips.

"Thanks. I guess I get to talk to Logan Miller all alone, then."

"Is that what you're doing with your day?" she asked.

"That and other things to make up for yesterday, yes. I figured someone should go and talk to him and tell him about Hannah. I don't want him sitting there, holding out hope if she's alive. Plus, I need to talk to his lawyers and make sure that they understand the manner of Hannah's death. He couldn't have done it, right?"

"Right, time of death was yesterday. He didn't kill her."

"So, all they'll have to worry about is Lidia Hobbs." Darek needed to call Bay and hoped that this time, the motherfucker would answer his phone.

"Well, I'll see you," Lizzy said. "I'll try to call at lunch, and if I'm close, maybe we can meet up?"

"I'd love that." Darek wanted her so badly, but he had to let her go to work. "Did you ever think about tomorrow night? We could have a nice dinner in this beautiful kitchen." He waved his hand around as she walked to the living room and then to the front door.

"I'm sure we can, and I'll let you know soon. I just don't know what this case is going to take. Maybe I won't have any time."

"Okay, fair enough." He followed her to the door and then gave her one last long kiss before she left.

Darek took his time getting dressed, preparing to spend his day at the penitentiary talking with Bay and Logan. He knew that both needed to know what was going on with Hannah. Their main focus should not only be on his defense for Lidia's murder, but Logan needed to deal with Hannah's loss, too. Darek also wanted to get a feel for their reactions to Hannah's death. He needed to know if either one of them had anything to do with it, especially Bay.

Darek headed out to the car and tried to call Bay again, hoping the man could meet up with him.

One ring and Bay's voice sounded on the other end. "You know, now that I'm not representing you, you can stop calling me all the time."

"I just thought you should know that we found Hannah Halston." He started his car and pulled out onto the road.

"You did, did you?" Bay's tone told him he wasn't expecting a call about Hannah, though he could have been wrong.

Darek decided to tell him what they knew. "Yes, and she's been murdered."

"Boy, that killer is really on a roll."

Darek turned and entered the freeway. "No, Bay. We're not sure this was the killer. It was a pretty messy job, so we're suspecting someone with interest in the case took her. Are you sure you haven't seen Hannah lately?"

"If you're asking if I killed her, Darek, the answer is no. That's not my style. When I do a job, I like things nice and tidy." His voice was tight, and Darek could tell he was insulted.

"I'm sure you do, but I had to ask. Someone kept her chained up since she went missing, and we have reason to believe that they broke her neck while trying to suffocate her. The coward couldn't even look her in the eyes."

"Very interesting. Where did they find her?"

"In the river. A couple of homeless men saw the dump and told us that it was two men in a black car. Whoever it is, they aren't making my fucking job any easier. I'm on my way to see Logan, by the way. Thought you might want to know, and if you want to meet up with us, here's your heads up."

"I can't. I have something to take care of, but I'll go see him later. You know, he's going to lose it when you tell him. He's probably going to want to confess."

"He won't want to talk, Bay. He's sacrificed too much already for that secret."

"I'm just warning you, friend. Be ready for it. Because when he starts threatening, I'm going to have to handle it, and neither one of you are going to like it." The phone went dead.

Darek drove the rest of the way to the prison, where he checked in and waited on Logan to be sent down.

"Darek. How's it going, man?" He grinned big, and it was good to see he still had all of his teeth. Logan's hair had been buzzed, but other than that, he looked good and healthy.

"Hey, Logan. How are they treating you?"

"Good, I'm actually making friends and keeping out of trouble, but I know Bay is pulling some strings for me."

"Well, I have good news and terrible news."

The grin faded from his face. "Just tell me."

"We found Hannah. She was killed and dumped in the river." Darek wasn't going to offer anything more to the man unless he asked him the right questions. He didn't need anything screwing with the investigation, and he held his breath for Logan's reaction.

"Fuck!" Logan punched the table. The guard on duty walked over, and Darek waved him away.

"I'm sorry, man. I wish I had better news, but you had to know that this was the most likely outcome."

"Bay had said that maybe she'd run. That's why I was still holding out hope."

"Well, the bright side, if there is one, is that she was killed the night before last, so we know that it wasn't you. And since we don't have anything but your false confession regarding her, there's a chance we could get you released."

Logan shook his head. "No way. I'm not leaving. I'll tell your boys that I killed Lidia if I have to."

"Why be stuck in here?" Darek asked. "You're not any safer. Trust me." He knew that Bay could pull the plug on him at any time.

"I can't face it, Darek. I can't go back out there and face a world where Hannah and Lidia belong, knowing I'll never see either one of them again."

Darek wished he could talk some sense into him, but he knew it wasn't going to happen today.

"Take care, man. And watch your back. Even Bay's capable of putting a knife in it."

Darek got up to leave, but Logan stopped him. "Hey, if she just died, where has she been?"

"Evidence shows she was chained up and held captive," Darek said. "We don't know where yet."

"Did she have symbols, too?" Logan had felt particularly bad about the marks since he'd been the one to make the brands. Darek wished he could reassure him, but he chose to be honest instead.

"Yes, yours and her brother's."

Tears filled Logan's eyes, and Darek walked away to let him grieve. He was on his way to his car when he decided to pull out the burner phone and send a message.

He typed the words: *I don't think you killed Hannah Halston.*

A moment later as he started his car, the killer replied: *Smart man.*

25

BAY

B ay watched Finn apologize over the phone to Wes Finkle. He explained that the artist could keep the deposit, but the film was on hold until he could get his life straightened out back in LA. It seemed the call was going well, and Finn, despite his failure, seemed to be in good spirits.

That was about to change.

Bay's conversation with Darek Blake had angered him. Knowing that Finn had not been able to follow simple instructions had Bay wanting to strangle him. As soon as Finn said goodbye and hung up the phone, Bay approached him. "I talked to the police today. They found a body down in the river. Hannah Halston."

Finn's eyes widened. "Already?"

"What the fuck do you mean, already? As if they were supposed to find her at all? I gave you and Lou specific instructions, so I want to know what happened. Every. Fucking. Detail."

Someone had dropped the ball, and while he thought that Lou had a lot to do with it, which was why the man had called him and told him that Finn had done a shitty job, Finn should have made sure that things were done the right way.

Finn looked terrified. "There wasn't a bag of concrete mix in the garage. Since it was midnight, we weren't able to go and buy any. We had nothing to use except for a few bricks, but those didn't work. They weren't heavy enough."

Bay was tired of hearing excuses. He had hoped that by keeping Finn close, he'd be able to use him as a scapegoat. Bay figured he'd get his hands dirty, make him feel secure, and then when the time was right, throw him under the bus, but the guy was about as useless as tits on a boar, as Bay's father used to say.

"Did they say anything else?" Finn asked, shaking like a leaf. "Do you think they'll be able to put me at the scene?"

"That depends. They know it's the work of an amateur, but as long as you didn't leave any DNA, say on her clothes when you were suffocating her, then you should be okay. Did you leave a mess, Finn?"

"I don't know. I tried not to, but she just kept talking. She wouldn't shut up. She made me angry, and I hit her."

"You left your DNA on her, didn't you?" Bay asked. "Once they comb her body for clues, they'll look at her clothes. One hair, one piece of skin under her nails, one tiny trace of anything." He wanted Finn to worry, to wonder if he was going to be in trouble. Bay needed him on edge to test him one more time. Make or break.

"I just did what you told me to do," Finn said. "I thought that you'd keep me safe."

"You're worried about yourself, but what about me? What about the others? If you get caught, it could lead right back to me. To all of us." Bay knew he had his own bases covered, but he liked the head fuck that he was giving Finn.

Finn's wide eyes were ringed red, and he crossed the room, seeking comfort. "I'm sorry, Bay. I didn't think she'd be found. Tell me what to do now."

"You go. You get your ass back to California, and you hope that nothing leads back to my doorstep because if it does, you're the one who will face the music."

"I'm sorry." He tried to reach for Bay, but Bay pushed him away. He wasn't into Finn like he'd made him think. The only physical contact had been minimal, and only to coax Finn into thinking Bay wanted more. Making him think he had a chance was the only way he was going to solve his Hannah problem.

The woman had become more and more violent, and it had become obvious that she wasn't going to conform for her own good. Bay knew he couldn't risk allowing her to turn on him, and he was starting to think the same thing about Finn and Logan.

The two of them, along with Darek, had tried to keep him out of the loop at every recent turn, and Hannah had sung enough that he knew she had almost turned them against him. The fact that Logan had messed up and told her all of the Zodiacs' secrets had sealed her death warrant, and it amused him to make Finn do it. But now, he was tired of playing. He had to send a final message, not only to Darek Blake but to the killer. Both of them needed to know who was really in control.

"Just go home, Finn. Get your shit straight, and maybe you can come back to me when you're really ready to be the man I need."

Finn's jaw dropped. "But I did everything you said. I've always tried to please you, Bay. You haven't even held up your end of things once, and frankly, I'm beginning to think you're never going to. Hannah was right. You use my love against me."

Bay laughed. The fact that he was just figuring this shit out was sad. "Then maybe you should just stay in Cali. Find you a nice girl and settle down. I'm sure she can give you what you need. Maybe Edie will take you back."

"She's pregnant, you know?"

"Congratulations," Bay said. "Maybe you'll figure out how to be a man and a father."

Bay couldn't get over that Finn hadn't told him, that he'd been willing to stay in New York away from his child so he could become Bay's lover. Not even his exclusive lover, but a side piece that was third string at best. What a fool. There was no way he'd ever abandon his child, and if Lila ever tried to take off with their baby, he'd put her in the ground, too.

Finn met his eyes. "You were never going to be with me, were you?"

"I guess you'll never know." Bay shrugged, hoping the not knowing would eat at him for the rest of his days. "I'll have Lou drive you to your car."

"Thanks."

"Hey," Bay said. "It's the least I can do before I leave."

"You're leaving?" Finn was insulted, and Bay thought it was amusing.

"I have clients to see. I have a career, remember?" He liked to rub it in since Finn had told him about how his own parents wanted him to pursue law or medicine.

With that, he readied himself to go and made arrangements for Finn's departure. When Lou showed up, he patted the man on the back and whispered in his ear. "Call me when it's done and bring me his phone."

He left without blinking an eye and then went to his car, knowing that by the end of the day, he would have fewer problems to deal with.

He drove down to the prison, and after checking in, he went to the meeting room to wait for Logan. He made sure he was in a private room with one guard and no video. He had a feeling that he was going to be right about the man's attitude, but he had to see for himself before he jumped to conclusions.

Even though he knew his next move was due, he had to see Logan before he made it.

"I know what you're going to say," Logan said when he arrived, with hair buzzed and looking more like a man on the inside than he had the last time Bay had seen him.

"And what's that?"

"Hannah's gone," Logan said. "You wouldn't happen to know anything about that, would you?"

"Why would I?"

"Yeah, right. I know you, Collins. You knew she was going to take you down, so you moved first. You always move first."

"I always move last, too, which is why you should watch your attitude. Besides, don't think I don't know that you were trying to shut me out. I know all about it. I know you told her everything and that she used you. Because you're weak. So weak you had to pull that desperate move to take off your brand. You got sloppy trying to go on your own. You're nothing but a traitor, Logan. Did you think it was smart to try and leave me out of the loop?"

"Not everything is your business, Bay."

"No, but you don't mind it when it is, do you? You love the benefits of my connections, of my money. It's all good when I can do things for you. You're no better than the others. As a matter of fact, you're worse because you couldn't even stay true to the group."

"Removing my mark had nothing to do with remaining true to the group. I did it for Hannah. You might have silenced her, but you can't stop me. I'm in here, and you're out there."

Bay nodded. "You're right. I can't touch you. You're really smart, Finn. Do you want to know what Hannah said at the very end? She said she still cared about you. That she was going to get free and tell the police everything so she could save you. She wanted to have a life with you. Buy a house and have some children. She had a really pretty picture in her mind, and I really hope it was the last thing she saw."

"You son of a bitch!" Logan jumped from his seat and came across the table, but the guard came in and grabbed him just as Bay was backing up. "I'll kill you! I'll make sure the police know everything you've done!" The guard got him in a headlock, and he gasped for his breath.

"Goodbye, Logan. I'm afraid I'm no longer going to be able to be your lawyer. There's no help for someone as sick as you." He turned to the guard. "Take him out of here. He's lost his mind."

Bay turned and gathered his briefcase. Then, as he walked out of the room and through the building, he took out his phone. Once he was outside the building, he walked out to his car and made a call. He leaned back in his seat and waited for someone to answer.

When he heard the voice on the other end, he had two words to say: "It's time."

The line went dead, and as Bay started his car, he knew that the task would be finished as soon as Logan returned to his cell block. Accidents happened every day in prison. Lucky him.

OTHER BOOK BY WL KNIGHTLY

ABOUT THE AUTHOR

WL Knightly is a thriller/murder mystery co-writing pen name for USA Today Best Selling Authors Lexy Timms and Ali Parker.

When she's not writing, Lexy can be found dealing in Antique Jewelry and hanging out with her awesome hubby and three kids.

Ali is a CPA turned fiction writer who is married to her best friend and lives in Texas. She spends her days writing and chasing three kiddos around the house.

The two friends met years ago when they both started writing and publishing in various young adult genres and needed a critique partner. The rest is history...

Made in the USA
Monee, IL
05 May 2022